BLAST FOR BLAST

"Come on!" Frost yelled to Akbar, racing down into the defile beyond the trees. Gunfire was heavy now from the far side where the six marksmen were. Frost aimed into the same target area as he paused in the trees, spraying the Soviet troopers below, the muzzle of his assault rifle bucking up, held in control by his aching arms. Then the rifle fired again, his ears splitting with the ringing of the explosions as more of the mines were set off. Trees fell across the road now, but one of the gas trucks was moving.

Frost ran forward twenty yards and dropped, ramming a fresh stick into the CAR-16, firing it into the windshield of the gas van. The glass shattered, the van lurching over the downed tree blocking its path. The van started to tip over, to roll, fire gushing from its gasoline tanks now as a rifle grenade blasted it.

Frost pushed himself to his feet, running now toward the killing ground. Akbar shouted to him, the AK-47 held high in his left fist, the sword high in his right. . . .

MORE EXCITING READING!

#15

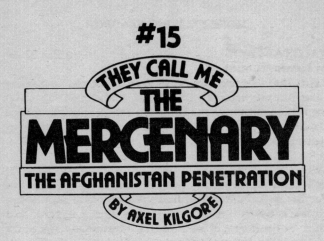

THEY CALL ME
THE
MERCENARY
THE AFGHANISTAN PENETRATION
BY AXEL KILGORE

ZEBRA BOOKS
KENSINGTON PUBLISHING CORP.

ZEBRA BOOKS

are published by

KENSINGTON PUBLISHING CORP.
475 Park Avenue South
New York, N.Y. 10016

Printed in the United States of America

For Ron Mahovsky—Hank Frost's armorer and my own—and one fine friend. All the best . . .

Chapter One

They looked like ghosts which floated across the hard packed gray and brown speckled mud. But they were women, Frost knew—white-veiled head to toe in the Moslem custom of Chadari. The veil formed a tiny, crosshatched window over the approximate area of the eyes through which they viewed the world and viewed him. He remembered the time he had first met his green-eyed, blond-haired Bess* and how she had been forced to pose as the veiled daughter of a Moslem merchant to escape an African dictator and a rogue mercenary commander. The one-eyed man felt a smile cross his lips, then as if to pull him back to the present, to the street market in Kohat, Pakistan, he felt Margaret Jenks tug at his sleeve.

"Hank, I think there's somebody following us. Hank!"

Frost nodded to her, saying nothing but instead touching at her left hand which was hooked inside his right elbow. He didn't glance over his shoulder— because he knew she was right.

Since leaving Karachi in search of information on Matt Jenks, they had been followed. That it was

*See THEY CALL ME THE MERCENARY #1, The Killer Genesis

perhaps the KGB had not escaped him either. Jenks had been Frost's friend in Vietnam and over the intervening years they had contacted each other twice. Jenks had been as fine a Green Beret as the Army could produce, yet had been disillusioned in Vietnam and left it all behind him. Disillusionment was something Matt Jenks had shared with many. He had worked the intervening years as a bush pilot in Alaska, a life he had left once to serve his country in the war. But then something had happened. Jenks had taken a faraway event personally, Frost thought. It had been the Soviet invasion of Afghanistan. His nineteen-year-old son, Bart, had helped Margaret with the flying service when Matt had left it this one more time. Matt had gone to fight the Soviets. His last letter out had reached Margaret Jenks three weeks earlier, dated six months earlier than that and no one she had been able to contact seemed able or willing to help her determine his fate.

Frost had been having dinner with Bess in their apartment outside Atlanta when the overseas call had come in from Karachi. The one time Frost had met Margaret Jenks he had gotten the distinct impression she hadn't liked him—not at all. But the phone call had been clear enough—Frost was her last hope to find out about Matt Jenks.

Frost and the woman turned a corner now into another street identical to the last—even the pattern of mud spots seemed so. Fruits and vegetables, many of which the one-eyed man could not identify, lay out from the fronts of the falling-down, tin-roofed market buildings themselves, puddles of murky water within easy splashing range of the wares themselves and the leathery faced men who hawked them in a language Frost did not understand. In contrast to the mud-packed street and the ghostly women and ragged men who walked it, power and telephone cables were inter-laced overhead, as if the airspace had entered the twentieth century while the ground and the people who walked it had not.

"Hank, they're getting closer. Hank!"

Frost again said nothing, turning then from the center of the street toward some of the shops. A light wind blew, a curtain parting in a doorway, and through the door in gray light suffused with meager sun, he could see a woman—her face oddly unveiled—weaving on a giant loom.

"Here—look out for the mud," Frost cautioned Margaret Jenks absently, helping her to outstep the confines of the straight skirt she wore and cross a pud-dle in the street.

A glass case, a row of glass cases, he realized—these fascinated him.

"My God," Margaret Jenks whispered beside him. The sound of her breath sucking in was audible over the rumblings and murmured conversations of the marketplace.

"An outdoor gunshop," Frost told her, not looking at her. He still disliked her—perhaps because he knew she disliked him still.

In one of the glass cases were loaded clips and maga-zines and loose cartridges for everything from Russian 7.62s to British .303s. A scale was behind the glass case into which he stared. He imagined the scale might be for weighing the ammo, a convenient way of selling it loose. Shotgun shells, various brands and calibers of

9

handgun ammunition—all ready for anyone who wanted to buy it.

"Pakistan isn't all bad," Frost noted sincerely. He moved on to the next case—pistols and revolvers. There were several Smith & Wesson Model 10 M&Ps, with varying degrees of blue remaining, and one nickel-plated with pearl grips, the pearl looking genuine enough even to the crack near the heel of the butt in the pearl itself. Berettas—the 1934 in 7.65mm and 9mm Corto or .380. There was a solitary Beretta Brigadier as well, the single column, single-action Model of 1951 in 9mm Parabellum, almost brand new. Lugers—he doubted any had matching serial numbers—and even a Broomhandle Mauser with a big red "9" denoting the caliber carved into the grip plate.

"Isn't bad at all," he said again, wishing he somehow could purchase the Lugers, the Broomhandle and then be able to import them legally to the U.S. and turn a handy profit. He shrugged, knowing he couldn't in any likelihood. Good Spanish Star autos and several less desirable German-made revolvers were in the next case, along with a Government Model .45. He studied the latter pistol. Its "Parkerized" phosphate finish was worn and it was "U.S." stamped.

He looked up from the case, a boy of no more than fifteen staring at him from the other side.

"Speak any English?" Frost asked, lighting a Camel in the blue-yellow flame of his battered Zippo windlighter.

"Little English, yes."

"How much—the .45?"

"Wait." The boy turned and stepped back through the curtain into the area where a moment earlier Frost had seen the unveiled and pretty woman weaving. A man appeared, seeming incredibly old, perhaps even more so in the sharper contrast between him and the young boy who now stood slightly behind him.

"Dollars?"

"Dollars," Frost nodded. "The .45 and a couple of spare magazines."

"Maga—"

"Clips," Frost nodded.

"Clips—yes?"

"And maybe a pound of ammo. You know—sixteen ounces if you understand that?"

"Pound—yes. Understand pound. Clips, pound of ACPs and gun. Two hundred American—yes?"

Frost didn't answer for a moment, cupping his hand over his cigarette in the light, cold mist that was beginning to fall. He could probably get the guy down a lot in price, he thought. He glanced up the street and saw five men, one European looking but swarthy-faced with a brushy mustache; the other four were Pakistani or trying cleverly to look that way. Like the man to whom he spoke now, they wore creamy white turbans bound around their heads, baggy trousers, heavy sweaters, and one wore what looked like a muffler around his neck. All four wore blanketlike shawls across their shoulders and wrapped around their upper bodies. Frost hunched his own shoulders in the brown leather bomber jacket he wore.

"Okay—two hundred American. Lemme see the gun first."

"Good gun—carried by General Patton once maybe."

"No shit," Frost nodded as the man unlocked the case and reached inside and withdrew the .45. The man

11

handed him the pistol and Frost jacked back the slide, the slide stop holding with the empty magazine in place. Frost thumbed down the slide stop, the slide homing forward. When he shook the gun it rattled. Twenty-five yards or less, he thought, likely a lot less. He'd used GI .45s like this one before. The guns were no match for even the poorest specimen of commercial Colt, these latter inherently accurate in the right hands. He worked the magazine release button. The feed lips didn't seem too mauled and there was the right tension when he depressed the follower with the little finger of his right hand. The grip safety worked, and he raised the thumb safety, then tried the trigger. The hammer didn't fall. "So far so good," he murmured. He looked up at the old man across the counter from him. "Still looking," he smiled to the man. He dropped the safety and drew the slide back, then raised the pistol skyward, water dropping on it and his face as the mist increased into a light rain. He inserted his thumbnail through the ejection port, bouncing light off the nail to try to see down the bore. There was rifling left—he could see that—and not any noticeable pitting.

Frost shrugged. "One hell of a pistol, friend. Two hundred American it is. Now let me see those spare magazines you've got. The clips."

"Clips. Yes—two clips."

"Three clips, plus the one in the gun."

"Two clips."

"You want two hundred American? Then three clips."

The old man nodded, saying something to the boy who started to reach into the ammo cabinet and with what looked like a rounded brass trowel scoop out .45

ACP hardball.

Frost began to check through the half dozen magazines the man put on the counter. One had feed lips that looked as though someone had hit them with a ballpeen hammer. One had a spring that didn't rise. But he found three good ones.

Frost eyed the five men who had followed him. They were watching him intently.

He smiled at them.

The boy was starting to pour the ammo into a cloth sack and Frost reached across the counter and stopped him, taking the ammo by handfuls from the scale and inspecting each cartridge. He tossed several away; they were hopelessly corroded, one even with a primer indentation. A hangfire no one had thrown away.

"Not these," Frost said to the boy. "And keep your hand off the scale when you weigh. Like buyin' fish in a bad neighborhood with you."

The boy looked at him, then at the old man.

The old man again said, "Two hundred American?"

Frost nodded and again in the unintelligible-sounding language the old man instructed the boy and the boy dug into the ammo pile once more. Frost began peeling twenties out of his money clip, stopping in mid-count to check the ammo. The new cartridges would likely have given the people at any of the major U.S. ammo manufacturers fits, but seemed serviceable in appearance.

He finished counting the money out and took the pistol.

"Lemme use your counter a second, huh?"

He didn't wait for an answer, instead began loading the three spare magazines and the one in the gun. He opened the slide again, dropping a round into the chamber, then worked the slide stop to run the slide forward, then upped the safety. He inserted one of the magazines after first whacking the spine of the magazine against the palm of his hand to seat the cartridges.

He looked at the old man, saying, "Enjoyed doing business with you, sir."

Frost turned toward the five men as he stuffed the pistol under his bomber jacket. He was likely violating a number of local laws—but staying alive was more important.

"Margaret? Let's keep walkin'." He looked at her, her face ashen, then added, "Maybe I can buy ya a rug!" He smiled but she didn't smile back.

Switching to her right side so his right hand would be free, he guided her down the street. If the directions he'd gotten were correct, beside the gatelike structure at the far end of the street would be the shop of Zulfikar Ali Pir, the one confirmed contact of Matt Jenks in Pakistan. Frost looked behind him once, feeling both guilty and perplexed about leading these five men to Pir's establishment. If they were KGB, they likely knew of Pir. But then why were they letting Frost go there? Too many people in the streets?

"This Mr. Pir—will he have word on Matt do you think, Hank?"

"We wouldn't be going there otherwise," Frost told her, trying to sound pleasant when he spoke with her but never quite achieving it. She was a pretty woman in her middle forties, wisps of gray in the otherwise almost unnaturally dark hair. Her hair was uncovered and drawing stares ranging from menace to incredulity from the faces of the Moslem men they had passed in the market.

Two women, one with a little boy tugging at the rear of her Chadar, were walking down the center of the street and Frost guided Margaret Jenks around them. The woman with the little boy was apparently better off than her veiled friend because of the better quality of the veil and the embroidery at the hem. And unlike the companion and the other women in the street, her veil was not white, but a deep gray.

"How can they stand to go around like that?" Margaret Jenks asked in a stage whisper.

Frost shrugged. "Probably has its advantages. You know, no time to do their hair, whatever. Who's gonna see?"

"Ohh," she almost groaned.

Frost decided he would stop trying to be cordial.

They stopped beside the shop nearest the gate and Frost looked at the faded sign near the wooden door, the wood there rough and unpainted. "Looks prosperous, huh?" Frost remarked, not caring if she answered. He looked behind him, not seeing the five men—this worried him.

The one-eyed man knocked on the closed wooden door, the wood rough under his knuckles.

The door swung inward. Rain was falling more heavily now, the shoulders of Margaret Jenks' trench-coat wet with it and dark-stained against the khaki coloring of the fabric. Frost could feel water dribbling down the back of his neck inside the turned-up collar of the bomber jacket.

"Let's go inside." He started in ahead of her, calling, "Mr. Pir? Zulfikar Ali Pir? Hello?"

He could feel the woman beside him, hear her breathing. Gray light filtered through air between the ceiling and the walls of the shop, but beyond that almost total darkness as the door slammed behind them with a gust of wind.

"I'm worried—I—"

Frost cut her off. "Good—plenty to be worried about, Margaret." The one-eyed man reached inside the bomber jacket, finding the shape of the unfamiliar pistol's butt and pulling the pistol out of his waistband. He could hear two things in the shop beyond the drumming of rain on the tin roof—the loud, gritty click of the safety on the Government Model going down under his thumb and the heavy breathing of the woman standing beside him in the darkness. He didn't hear his own breathing because he was holding his breath. He let it out in something like a long sigh.

"Stand here—don't move. Just stand here, Margaret, and for God's sake don't talk."

Frost felt her hands tugging at his left arm, then felt them no more as he stepped forward into the darkness. His right elbow was locked close to his side, the .45 rock steady in his right fist and drawn close to his body so a kick or the downswing of a club couldn't knock it away. With the darkness, fifty people could have been standing shoulder-to-shoulder around him no more than six feet away and he wouldn't have seen them.

"Hank!"

"Shut up, Margaret!" he rasped. He took another step forward, feeling something against his foot and stopped. "Holy shit," he murmured.

He reached into his pocket for the Zippo, flicked it open with his left hand and moved the light it afforded

16

in a sweeping motion around the room. There was no one in the shop except himself and Margaret Jenks—no one living, at least. He stooped over. He had almost tripped on the body of a man, the throat slit ear-to-ear in the yellow-tinged glow of the lighter. And beside the man—evidently Mr. Pir from the contorted face which matched the description—was a young girl. The veil being gone shocked him suddenly. The women of strict Moslem faith wore it to guard their virtue. Her virtue was gone—like the veil. Visibly missing. The throat was slit, as was Mr. Pir's, but another slit bothered him, between her spread thighs. As he bent over her he could detect the bleachlike smell of semen.

The five men, not watching him but shepherding him to the shop.

"Margaret, there's a dead man here and a dead woman."

"Oh, my God—what—"

"Shut up, Margaret. The woman is a young girl. She was raped, either before or after. Probably mattered to her, but doesn't to us. She was Moslem. This is a set-up."

Frost stood up and closed the lighter, trying to control his breathing, summon up "chi" like his pal Ron Mahovsky did before a martial arts confrontation. Frost closed his eye, seeing a mental picture of what would be outside. The European-dressed man would likely be absent, or at the far rear of the crowd, the other four dressed as Pakistanis indistinguishable from the crowd they would have gathered—the mob.

And he knew what the words would be though he couldn't understand the language. "An infidel has violated the virgin daughter of Zulfikar Ali Pir!" Then

17

there would be various local equivalent references to Frost's relationship with his mother, his mother's occupation and the like. "Shit," he snarled, turning back to face Margaret. He couldn't leave her behind. If the mob had no interest in her the European-dressed man and his friends would.

"Margaret, listen. When we get outside, chances are there'll be a mob of people out there blaming me, maybe both of us for this."

"But—"

"Sure—we'll just call that medical examiner guy on television and he'll establish the time of death as before we entered the shop. But by then, I'll be dead and you'll be worse off probably. We're gonna walk out of the door, smile at the nice people and try to run like hell. Through those gates and toward the government buildings and the police station or barracks—whatever the hell it is."

"But that's a mile. I was never any good at running, even when I was a girl."

"I was never a girl so I don't know." He waited— there was no laugh. Not even a little one. "Hope you improved since then, kid." Frost walked over to stand beside her, again controlling his breathing, trying to summon energy from inside himself, to focus his mind and body on running, fighting—whatever would be needed to stay alive.

He didn't say anything, but started with her toward the door, holding her right hand in his left. For an instant he thought about Margaret's shoes—low-heeled, sensible enough looking. He was glad of that. His own sixty-five-dollar shoes squished a little inside.

He wondered if it were the rain or that he was sweating as badly from the soles of his feet as from the palms of his hands.

He pulled the door in toward him with the same hand that held the pistol.

Outside the door were faces—a sea of faces. Some were bearded and turbanned above the furrowed brows and scowling mouths, some with the little Moslem versions of the yarmulka caps, young faces, angry-eyed.

No one in the crowd spoke, the eyes watching him.

"Anyone speak English?"

There was a voice from the back of the crowd, the English slightly accented. "I do, Captain Frost."

It was the European, the one he'd mentally labeled as KGB.

"You did this," Frost sang out. "Right?"

"Not actually me—but you're more right than wrong. And I am the only one who speaks English. I also speak their language. Want to listen?"

Frost didn't want to listen. The man—KGB Frost was certain now—called out in a sing-song and nasal voice some things that in any language would have sounded foul, Frost decided. The looks on the faces of the crowd turned from anger and hatred to murder.

"Run!"

Frost fired his pistol into the mud near the feet of the nearest man, shouts and yells and what could only have been curses starting. The one-eyed man saw a break in the crowd to his left and started for it, pulling Margaret Jenks beside him. A massive white turban-clad man with a bristling black beard stepped in front of him.

19

Frost snapped the pistol out in his right hand, hammering the butt of it into the nameless man's jawline. The man rocked back, Frost's left knee snapping up, into the gut rather than the crotch, doubling the man forward. Pushing him back, for the first time Frost heard Margaret Jenks screaming. Frost tugged at her hand, pulling her forward with him, hands reaching out to him from the crowd, curses and shouts assailing his ears, then a pistol shot.

The one-eyed man sidestepped two other men, wheeling, seeing a Pakistani shoving people aside as he pushed through the mob, a large-framed revolver—maybe an N-Frame Smith, Frost thought—in his upraised right hand. The Pakistani shoved a Chadar-clad woman to the ground and leveled the handgun.

Frost's right arm snaked out, the pistol in his hand like an extension of his body, the sights something he didn't have time for and wouldn't have trusted anyway. The .45 bucked once in his hand. The Pakistani with the revolver looked startled but as best Frost could tell, unhurt. But the gunfire, aimed at someone, rather than just into the ground, was having a marvelous effect on the crowd—breaking up the mob in almost as many directions as there were people to run. The Pakistani pointed the revolver again, swatting aside another man, firing. Frost dodged left, pushing Margaret Jenks with him, then fired the .45. He missed, but saw the bullet smash into a puddled surface five yards behind the Pakistani and three feet to the left. Elevation was okay, Frost decided—he needed more windage or lateral deflection. He felt stupid doing it as the Pakistani made to fire again, but the one-eyed man aimed the pistol three feet to the right of the Pakistani's left shoulder and fired. The Pakistani's face contorted. The body spun, the revolver discharging again, but into the air, the body already falling.

Frost looked down at the .45 and grinned, then grabbing Margaret Jenks' hand started running again. She was shouting something and he looked at her. "You killed that man!"

Frost decided that the woman definitely had keen powers of observation. They were through the gate and into a massive square, the sky suddenly opening and the cold rain streaming down in torrents as they kept running.

"Across the square—hurry!" Behind him again he could hear the rumblings of the mob.

Opposite the square Frost could see another gate at the end of a funnel-shaped street and he ran for it, turning once, the mob closing on him. Absently, he thought that the angry, blood-crazed Pakistanis would make great Olympic sprinters. They were gaining on him. He turned, pushing the woman behind him, firing the pistol high over the heads of the crowd, pumping the trigger again and again. He slowed their headlong lunge after him. The .45's slide locked open.

Frost dumped the magazine into the mud and started to run again, ramming another magazine up the well, working the slide stop down, hearing rather than seeing the slide running forward, stripping a fresh round into the chamber off the top of the magazine.

The street was close now, and Frost, his lungs and his shins aching, bent low into the run. Margaret Jenks panted beside him.

21

"I—I—I can't—can't run anymore! Hank!"

Frost looked at her once, shouting to her, "They'll rip your arms off and beat you to death with 'em if you don't!"

He felt her pace quicken beside him and he let go of her hand. He was almost into the funnel now, skidding on his heels suddenly in the mud, a second mob of Pakistanis running out of the tube of the funnel from the gates beyond. They were screaming and shouting, knives and clubs brandished in upraised hands.

"Aww, hell!" Frost rasped, wheeling around, the mob behind him, closing in.

Frost grabbed the woman and pushed her behind him.

"Hang in there, lady," he snarled, the .45 outstretched in his right fist like a wand. The rain fell so heavily now that the rivulets running down from his soaked hair almost blinded him. He ran the fingers of his left hand back through his hair, edging toward a row of vendors' stalls. The mob was stopped on both sides of him now, the fringes of each blending together at the center, a wedge blocking him.

"Hank, what'll we do?"

"What you mean we, paleface?" Frost snapped back.

"Hank!"

"Laugh, dammit—come on! We're gonna get ripped to pieces anyway. May as well have a good laugh. Laugh!" He was losing it, he realized—after all the brushes with death, this time he faced a mob of people he didn't even know trying to rip him apart for a crime he hadn't committed.

"Hell—come on!" He shouted it now to the crowd,

22

wishing he spoke enough of the language just to curse them out. "Come on, you no good bunch of—of—hell!"

Four men started from the center of the crowd, knives in their hands, the kind with curved blades that would be etched or engraved, the kind made for killing people or hacking down crops.

Frost hunched slightly forward, the pistol ready, a spare magazine clutched in his left fist—so that maybe he could load it in time to take out fourteen of them rather than just seven.

"Come on. Come on!"

The four came, almost as if they heard him. Frost's first finger edged against the trigger.

"Hank!"

"Shut up, Margaret!"

Frost watched the eyes of the four men, to see who would come at him first.

He picked the one on the far left, watched the knife hand as it twitched, then saw the run start.

Frost wheeled, pumping the .45. The man's body spun out, the knife flying into the mud, the body splashing after it. The other three were lunging for him. Frost swung the muzzle of the .45.

Shouts came from bullhorns, and suddenly the crowd was breaking up. Khaki-clad men with long white batons ran into the center of the mob, hacking at heads and backs and shoulders with the nightsticks.

Only one of the still-standing knife wielders was coming—despite the police.

Frost upped the .45's safety and dropped the pistol into the mud. He edged back, the police breaking up the mob, the last knife wielder fighting his way toward Frost still.

"Margaret, run up to a cop and surrender—now!"

She didn't move.

"Now, dammit!"

He felt Margaret's movement behind him in the same instant the man with the knife came for him. The one-eyed man sidestepped, the knife arm flashing past him. Frost half-wheeling right, snaked out his left foot in a Tae-Kwon-Do kick to the knife wielder's right forearm. The man lurched back, Frost trying a second kick, missing, almost losing his balance in the slick footing of the mud.

The knife wielder was coming again, curses spitting from his lips as he threw himself forward. Frost sidestepped, but so did the man with the knife, the blade making a slicing sound in the air as it arced past the one-eyed man's throat. Frost dodged his head back, away from the steel. His right foot snapped up and out, the instep hammering into the man's groin. Frost sidestepped as the knife hacked downward.

Frost edged back, the knife wielder turning, dropping the knife, reaching under his blanketlike shawl and pulling a small looking automatic from the folds of his clothes.

Frost started to dive for him, but sidestepped as a fusilade of shots opened up around him, the man's body dancing with them, the pistol falling forward out of his fist. The body lurched, then fell forward into the mud.

Hands grabbed Frost about the shoulders and he felt a nightstick hammer into his stomach, doubling him over, dropping him to his knees. In the mud beside the dead man the police had just shot, Frost could see clearly the little pistol. It was a Makarov—Soviet and brand-new looking.

"KGB." Frost said it to himself because he had decided that none of the police spoke English either. He hoped they got him up out of the mud, though.

Chapter Two

There were cops and then there were cops, Frost decided. These had evidently decided he was guilty of raping a Moslem woman and killing her, then killing her father when the man had tried to defend her. Frost had forgotten how many times one of the policemen had rapped him across the shins with a baton, or how many times another had rammed the baton like a knife into his abdomen. The pain in his abdomen now was intense, more so than it would have been except for the position he was in.

They had taken all his clothes except his underpants, shackled his ankles and his wrists, but run the links connecting the wrist bracelets around the links connecting his ankles. He sat now the only way he could. His knees were tucked almost under his chin and his arms extended between his thighs, his hands—slightly purple—between his ankles. His back ached. His shoulders ached and he could smell himself—smelling bad after vomiting the last time he'd been hammered in the guts with the nightstick. The mess hadn't been cleaned off him.

He'd kept shouting, "American!" until he was hoarse, or until one of the police had punched him in the face—he couldn't exactly remember it now. Where

Margaret Jenks was now was uncertain. He assumed at least she was being treated better.

Frost studied the floor of the cell—unable to raise his head enough to do more.

There was a rat on the far side by the metal door, shuffling along in the mud. The rat occasionally looked up, staring back. Frost hoped the rat had other things to do. If it started chewing on him there would be no way he could fend it off.

His breathing was getting more labored and this worried him, too. If the American who had raped the daughter of Zulfikar Ali Pir were to die in his cell, then the investigation would be closed.

And there was still Matt Jenks. Assuming Frost did get out of the cell—which he realized was a dimmer prospect by the second—with Pir dead, there was no lead to Matt Jenks at all.

Bess had been less than enthusiastic about him going. He was beginning to wish he'd listened to her and never left Atlanta. . . .

She was in his arms, her breasts naked against his chest, her nipples hot on his flesh, her hands searching him. He saw a warm smile traced on her face, deep smile lines or shallow dimples—he'd never known which—etched in the corners of her mouth as she raised her face, kissing him. . . .

Was it the rat? Something was tugging at him.

Frost opened his eye. The man with the penchant for ramming batons into abdomens was standing over him, a dangling ring of keys in his hands. The policeman bent down and undid the shackles on Frost's hands, easing Frost back against the wall. The one-eyed man let out a long hard sigh—the pain in his back, his kidneys aching, his shoulders burning and his stomach feeling like it was tied in knots.

Frost tried to flex his arms, slowly, as the policeman undid the shackles on Frost's ankles.

The policeman stepped back, looking down at Frost, the baton in a ring off a Sam Browne belt with an empty flap holster on the right side.

The policeman leaned down over Frost, the hands something Frost could feel under his armpits as the policeman started raising him to his feet.

"That tickles," Frost said, feeling his lips dry, cracked.

The policeman looked at him a moment, then smiled, saying nothing.

Frost reached out his right hand and closed his fist around the handle of the baton. As the policeman got him up to his feet, Frost wrenched out the baton, then stabbed it forward, into the policeman's gut. The policeman's hand loosened on him, and Frost crashed the baton down laterally across the shoulder blades. The policeman shouted something, Frost stumbling back against the wall as the policeman fell at his feet. Three more police poured into the cell through the open doorway, standing batons drawn, bracing him.

"Come on!" the one-eyed man rasped.

"I'm not certain that's really necessary, Captain Frost."

The three baton-armed men stepped aside. A man—American looking with red hair and shiny, almost polished complexion—stepped between them into the cell.

"I'm John Plaskewicz with the American Embassy. I was on my way to Islamabad when I heard about the

28

little mix-up here."

"It's the KGB. That's the little mix-up, Plasnewicz."

"Plaskewicz—with a "K." But if it is our Soviet friends, let's keep that our little secret for now." Plaskewicz wrinkled up his nose, then added, "Why don't we get you a bath and some clothes, then talk."

"Free to go?" Frost asked.

"As a bird."

"Even after slugging him?"

"I guess he had it coming. The chief here told me the man was occasionally overzealous in his treatment of prisoners."

"Good." Frost dropped the nightstick and kicked the unconscious man in the face with his bare right foot. "Good," he repeated, then started toward the cell door, almost tripping on the confused rat.

Chapter Three

"You're either a lousy shot or a good one. That young guy you plugged who had the knife—just before the cops came?"

"Yeah?"

"You nailed him in the right thigh, dropped him like a rock I understand. But he should be up and around in a little while. No permanent damage."

"Glad to hear it. All he was doing was trying to kill me."

"But because of a mistake."

"It wasn't any mistake. I was set up."

Plaskewicz lit a cigar. "That guy the cops plugged—hung around with known Soviet agents. Just like the other guy you shot back in the market."

"You gonna help Margaret Jenks and me or are you just going to talk?" Frost reached for his drink. It was lunchtime in Islamabad. The hotel restaurant's American food sounded promising, and the liquor tasted good. Frost knew that already. He was drinking scotch—the most expensive brand on the English-printed menu, since Plaskewicz had said he was buying.

"I said we're going to help—in the best way we can, at least."

"Matt Jenks is an American citizen," Frost said through a mouthful of cigarette smoke, exhaling it in a cloud across the table, combating the cigar the CIA man smoked.

"That doesn't always mean what it used to," Plaskewicz smiled. "You know—Teddy Roosevelt and his big stick."

"He was a good guy," Frost interrupted.

"Would have plunged the world into a nuclear war these days, I'm afraid," Plaskewicz smiled good-naturedly.

"Maybe," Frost shrugged, taking another sip of his drink, stubbing out his cigarette.

"Foreign policy is more complex."

"You still pretending you're a diplomat?"

"Because I said that? No—not at all. I just think that's obvious. As an intelligence-gathering arm of government, we only carry out policy. We do not make it."

"Different CIA these days, huh?" Frost laughed.

"Hardly—just a more conscientious approach to our basic mission. Less cowboying around if you know what I mean." Plaskewicz smiled.

Frost glanced at the black face of his Rolex Sea-Dweller. "Isn't Margaret Jenks coming?"

"No. I had the Embassy call her in for a report on yesterday's incident. I thought a private conversation between just ourselves would be more fruitful, Captain."

"Fruitful?" Frost rolled the word in his mouth a moment. "Fruitful—sure," and Frost nodded. His back still ached, but it always did after added strain was put on it. He remembered the operation he'd had after

31

escaping the drug warlords in the Burmese Golden Triangle.* He would never forget it.

"Matt Jenks wasn't just a volunteer, or a mercenary. He was working for us."

Frost looked at Plaskewicz across the rim of his glass. "Contract employee?"

"Yes, and an important one. Very important."

"That why Margaret Jenks couldn't get any word on him—or help, either?"

"As I said, diplomatic entanglements these days aren't quite so simplistic. We can't send a company of Marines in after him, or for that matter even a commando squad. We don't really know exactly where he is, anyway."

"Afghanistan, I bet." Frost smiled, sipping his scotch.

"Likely, but perhaps somewhere else by now—if he's alive. You see, each of us has a different interest here. Matt Jenks knew the risks and he took them anyway. You want to find out his fate, maybe even attempt to bring him out, I'd love that, personally. But what we have an interest in is far more important than Matt Jenks—or you."

"What—the Afghani war or the way the Russians are fighting it—or both?"

"More of the latter really." Plaskewicz looked up, then he smiled broadly, saying, "And we've been having a lot of rain here, too, Captain."

Frost glanced up. The waiter was within earshot, pushing a silver cart with silver serving dishes on it, steam condensed on the lids.

*See, THEY CALL ME THE MERCENARY #4, The Opium Hunter

32

"Yeah," Frost nodded. "That rain was really something. Here's our food. Would you look at that!"

Plaskewicz just smiled again. The waiter stopped the cart and a second man—not so elaborately dressed—joined him. The second man attended the dishes, the waiter doing the actual serving. It took too long. Frost was anxious to continue the real conversation with the CIA man.

The waiter and his assistant finally left, Plaskewicz saying, "Seems like the weather all over the world is getting unpredictable these days. Hate to be a weatherman. So anyway, Matt Jenks was getting both kinds of information for us—on the prosecution of the war and on Soviet weapons and tactics. They don't trot everything out in the May Day parade, you know."

"How'd he get the stuff out?" Frost asked, studying his steak for a moment before attacking it.

"A system of couriers, through the Khyber Pass, down here to Zulfikar Ali Pir. Then Pir would route it through Peshawar, then sometimes from Kamra to Havelian, sometimes to Rawalpindi, but either way into Islamabad. Jenks' last report was in code. And the code was intentionally garbled, difficult for us to crack. And he only made lateral allusions to the subject."

"What? What was the report dealing with?"

"I memorized the quote."

"Good for you," Frost smiled, spearing a piece of meat with his fork and tasting it. He'd had better.

"He talked about a new Soviet weapon—something he described as—and I quote him—capable of bringing the West to its knees if its testing is successful in Afghanistan. He was going to get more information, and he wasn't an alarmist. I know your service record, and after the war. You've worked with intelligence people enough—"

"To know they don't usually have any intelligence?"

"Very smart. I could say the same thing for ex-Special Forces guys turned mercenary."

Frost shrugged. "So make your point."

"My point is, we both know guys in this business who embroider on the truth, to make their reports sound that much more important. Especially contract agents working far away from any control."

"Matt wouldn't have done that," Frost said flatly.

"I agree—and that's what has me worried. Like I said, he was going to get more information for a subsequent report. That was almost three months ago. We didn't get up tight right away. Sometimes it's been thirty, maybe sixty days between reports. Unless Jenks had something to say, he didn't risk the life of a courier."

"Where was he?" Frost asked Plaskewicz.

"He was working with one of the six Mujahedin guerilla groups, beyond the Hindu Hush almost to Amu Darya. That's why he made infrequent reports. In those mountains there has been some of the worst fighting, some of the worst killing. Gas warfare—we know about that. Kids' toys that conceal anti-personnel mines. All of that. But whatever this is, Jenks saw it as worse. Parts of the report talked about it destroying Western armies on the ground and in the air. That's all we know."

"You think he's alive up there?" Frost asked, breathing a long sigh, setting down his fork and picking up his drink.

"I don't know. All of us have different speculations. My gut reaction is that he was captured or wounded so seriously that either way he can't get a message out. If he's been captured, he could still be up there. If he hasn't—well, God knows. But if the Communists did take him he could be back in Moscow by now, spilling his guts. You know how persuasive they can be at KGB headquarters, I understand."*

"Yeah, I know all right," Frost answered softly, lighting a Camel in the blue-yellow flame of his battered Zippo.

"Would you be willing to risk that again—to help out Matt Jenks or at least find out what he was killed for?"

"You want me to go up there." It wasn't a question, but a statement.

"I've got a man we've worked with before, one we trust. I'll send him with you. He can get along in all twenty major languages. He worked in the Mujahedin before he helped get his wife and kids out. He's from here originally—a Pathan from the Afridi tribe."

"The what?"

"It's the tribe that for generations has guarded the Khyber Pass. They are some of the toughest fighters in the world. Guns, knives, hands, rocks—anything."

"Sounds like my kinda guy," Frost smiled.

"Will you do it? There's fifty thousand dollars in it for you just to go up there. Another hundred thousand if you find out what Matt Jenks was talking about. Another hundred thousand on top of that if by some

*See, THEY CALL ME THE MERCENARY #14, The Siberian Alternative

35

miracle you could bring it back, or enough pieces of it or detailed photos—"

"So you could reproduce it?" What the world desperately needed, Frost thought ironically, was another weapon of mass destruction.

"If they've got it and it works, we need it. Will you do it? The money's good."

"I'd do it for free. And whatever happens, a hundred thousand dollars on top of that goes right now to Matt Jenks' wife and their son, Bart. Agreed?"

Plaskewicz said nothing for a moment, then nodded soberly. "Agreed. I can swing it."

"I'll need a lot of equipment, some weapons of my own that I can trust. All I had was that retread .45, and that's gone."

"If you hadn't dropped that, the local police would have shot you. A smart move."

"One thing—who was that son of a bitch from the KGB? The one who set me up?"

"We know him as Klaus Igorovitch—probably not his name, though. He's back in Kabul by now."

"Assuming the KGB has a better intelligence network here than you have there, as soon as I set out, he's going to know about it."

"More than likely," Plaskewicz nodded grimly.

"So besides your ordinary garden-variety hundred thousand Soviet troops to worry about, the rivalries between the six groups in the Majahedin—"

"You do your homework, Frost."

"I can even read and write a little. Sometimes I amaze myself."

"It'll be rough. And your chances of getting out alive are poor to none."

"I guess," Frost sighed heavily, stubbing out his cigarette and looking at his steak. The meat was cold. "I guess if somebody had asked Matt Jenks to come and get me out, he would have tried it." Frost took a sip of his drink, saying half aloud, "What am I gonna tell Bess?"

Chapter Four

The first call had been to Ron Mahovsky, head man of Metalife Industries and Frost's armourer and old friend. Frost wanted three more twenty-round extension magazines for the Metalifed High Power, six worked-over thirty-round magazines for the Colt AR-15/M-16 type rifle, and a wish of good luck. All but the latter was to be sent to Langley, Virginia, where CIA would get them into a diplomatic pouch for Islamabad.

The next call had not been that easy, Frost recalled, sipping a drink now at the hotel bar. Bess had been—he searched for the word, then smiled as he thought of it—"pissed." He couldn't tell her exactly where he was going but she knew—it was obvious. He told her he might be gone as long as twelve weeks, and she added he might be gone forever. She hadn't even asked why he was going.

Her anger calmed, she had simply said, "I love you. Get back here to me, Frost. I'm lonely without you." He had told her much the same, then hung up.

The next day had been spent in putting together equipment, going over intelligence reports and waiting for Bess's shipment of his Browning High Power and some other gear, as well as Mahovsky's shipment of the magazines. Meanwhile, Frost had gotten together with a Marine gunnery sergeant at the Embassy and had assembled one of his pet bastardized weapons—a commercial Colt CAR-15 with M-16 receiver parts. The result made a collapsible-stock, selective-fire assault rifle with a barrel length he could live with. They had clamped on a standard Colt 3X scope and mounts. At the police range in Islamabad—how Plaskewicz had connived permission Frost had no idea—Frost had zeroed the weapon as best he could on a fifty-yard position for hundred-yard use.

By the next morning, the equipment from the States had arrived and Frost had spent the morning and early afternoon checking everything one last time. He loaded magazines, sharpening the Gerber MkI boot knife, oiling his combat boots—all the details that needed doing and would kill time until meeting his guide.

He had drifted into the bar an hour before Plaskewicz was to pick him up, having gone to his room and changed first into Levis, his leather bomber jacket and his boots.

Every other man in the bar wore a tie, even the bartender, and Frost had felt a bit out of place. He thought about that as he sipped at his scotch. He could tell someone who asked, if anyone asked, that he was a rich eccentric. He wasn't rich—not really—but the eccentric part anyone would buy, just looking at him.

"Frost?"

The one-eyed man turned around, putting down his drink. It was Plaskewicz. "You ready?" Frost asked.

Plaskewicz nodded, Frost standing up and tossing down money on the bar and following Plaskewicz out. As they walked through the Oriental-carpeted lobby, Plaskewicz said, his voice almost as low as a whisper:

"Akbar Ali Husnain always feels confined in a car, that's why I'm hurrying."

"Akbar? That's the guy who's—"

"Yeah, he's the one," Plaskewicz said pleasantly, holding open the side door into the street, Frost stepping through. A black Cadillac waited at the curb, but no one sat inside except a chauffeur.

"I thought you said—"

"He's waiting in another car, outside Rawalpindi— not a long drive. Come on."

"The gear?" Frost asked, starting inside.

"It's already there, waiting," Plaskewicz answered, stepping in, the car already going into motion. "Now— we'll go over this a lot," Plaskewicz began. "There's a helicopter waiting outside Rawalpindi that'll drop you and Akbar just northwest of Peshawar—about twenty clicks from the Khyber Pass. There are two roads— one for trucks and one for camels. Now here's the way we've got it figured for you and Akbar to get across."

"Wonderful," Frost nodded, lighting a cigarette. He loved using other people's plans.

"Like I said, there are two roads. But you and Akbar aren't going to use either one. Hope you like rock climbing."

Chapter Five

The KG-99, which Bess had also shipped in for him along with the Metalifed High Power, was on a tight web sling across his back, under his Lowe Alpine Systems Loco Pack, the CAR-16—as he called his modified rifle—slung diagonally across his body and under his right arm. He carried the High Power under the heavy Navy peacoat; beneath the Cobra shoulder rig which carried the weapon he wore a heavy forest-green British Army pullover with cloth shoulder and elbow patches. The one-eyed man pulled the dark blue Navy watch cap lower on his head, flexing his fingers in his doubly thick gloves, waiting in a niche of rock.

Akbar Ali Husnain—Frost had caught sight of him only once since the Pathan had run along the ridge line to check for Soviet patrols. The man moved, Frost reflected, like a ghost.

Husnain had not been waiting in the car near the helicopter at all, but sitting cross-legged on the hood instead. Worn brown leather cartridge bandoliers crisscrossed his chest like a railroad sign, a startlingly well-preserved bolt-action Springfield '03 across his thighs. He had been hatless there in the milder temperatures away from the mountains through which the Khyber cut and through which conquerors had passed since the time of Herodotus. He was a historian, Herodotus was. Frost had read about him once.

At Husnain's belt, over the heavy black coat he'd worn, was a brown flap holster. Frost had yet to see the gun it carried but had pegged it as a revolver. Strapped across Husnain's back had been something which brought memories to the one-eyed man—a sword.*

The blade was perhaps as long as a man's arm—a tall man's arm—and the blade had a subtle curve like a samurai's katana sword, but seemed somehow larger. Husnain's eyes had lit with something akin to curiosity when he had noticed Frost eyeing the blade. As Husnain had sprung from the hood of the Cadillac, the sword flashed from his back, cutting a wide arc through the air, Husnain spinning like a ballet dancer, then coming to rest—his feet at stark angles, the right leg slightly bowed, the sword point down beside his right foot. And he had laughed, the bearded face seaming.

Less of the face was visible when Husnain had left to scout the ridge, a knit watch cap covering the close-cropped black hair; and covering the cap and swathing the face and neck was a gray burnoose.

Frost shifted position slightly, hearing something, starting to raise the muzzle of the CAR-16. But he saw Husnain twenty feet behind him, coming along below the ridge line.

"Your ears—they are good, Captain."

"Your feet are noiseless, Akbar."

"Ahh—it is the way to stay alive." Akbar's eyes were smiling as he settled himself into the niche of rock.

*See, THEY CAL ME THE MERCENARY #13, Naked Blade, Naked Gun

"There is our enemy now. There are no Soviet troops near enough to concern us, but this—" Akbar gestured toward the ridge line.

From the distance at least, the mountains looked almost naked in their grayness.

Frost took the Bushnell Armored 8x30s and peered through the right tube. He could see some vegetation, what looked to be many ledges and crevices. "I don't understand," Frost told Akbar, taking down the binoculars and recapping the lenses as he spoke.

"The Russians patrol here—always." He spat into the rocks. "If they see us, they can stay well below and fire at us. Each patrol unit has a sniper with it, for just such a purpose. We can fire back, but only delay ourselves and give the sniper a stationary target. Not good. We must be sure and fast—ask that Allah watch over us. Come, Captain." Akbar spat again, lighting a hand-rolled cigarette which he'd been making as he talked. The cigarette dangled from the left corner of his mouth.

Frost pushed himself to his feet and followed after, his right fist clenched tight on the CAR-16 pistol grip.

They had been resting in the defile of the ridge line, Afghanistan a blue haze below them and beyond the last cut of the pass. Akbar held the same cigarette in the corner of his mouth, dead there for hours. He finally removed it. White paper stuck in tiny bits to his dried lips, his mouth cutting into a grin, the teeth yellowed but straight.

"You looked strangely at my sword."

"Don't see too many men going into combat these

days with one. That's the reason."

"Ahh—this is true. That is why the sword is an advantage to me. Here," and Akbar Ali Husnain unfolded the wrap which covered him over his coat, then opened the coat itself. Frost was chilled to the bone in the wind. Under the coat Akbar wore a shoulder holster, a revolver—it looked like an old Smith & Wesson—under his left armpit, under the right armpit a knife. "A knife is good, but a sword can kill many. My father carried a sword proudly. Not this sword—my son will have that someday. And he will have this, maybe, when he fights. Two swords."

"When he fights," the one-eyed man repeated.

"I am Pathan. It is my life to fight. It will be his life. It is these mountains—they must be guarded. Today it is the Soviet Union, yesterday it was the Persians, the Greeks, the Turks. Tomorrow it will be someone else. But the mountains will be here then, and my son will be here, like my father was here."

"Why were you in Afghanistan—like Plaskewicz said?"

"To fight the Communists. But the Communists were getting too strong, and there was much danger for my wife and my sons and daughter. I brought them back. I have traveled much in Afghanistan since. And what of you? This man Jenks? He is a good friend?"

"He was, a long time ago. We fought in Vietnam together."

"Ahh—a war like this. But jungles and not mountains. You know war then."

Frost thought about the answer for a moment, but said nothing.

"Sometimes no words can be the best words. Come,"

and Akbar, his coat already re-buttoned, rose to his feet in one easy motion, folding the robe about him and hunching into a run. The one-eyed man climbed to his feet—stiff with the cold—and jogged after him. . . .

The ledge was perhaps twice the width of a broad-shouldered man. Frost walked stiff-legged half a pace behind Akbar as they descended the mountains. Beyond the lip of the ledge was a drop of what Frost judged at least fifteen hundred feet, perhaps more than that. Rotted wood jutted out at points from the ledge, slats covering it, expanding the width of the "road." The rock and the dirt were gray, but a lighter gray than the wood itself.

"Bad feelings, Captain—no Russians and there should be Russians."

"Isn't using the trail asking for it?" Frost asked for the umpteenth time since they had taken it two hours earlier.

"Could be. But to cross the mountains here without the trail would take three days. Too long. We will leave the trail in another four clicks, maybe less, depending." Husnain did not say what "depending" depended on, but simply moved the lightless cigarette in the corner of his mouth and shifted his Springfield on his right shoulder, walking on.

Frost fished in the outer pocket of the peacoat on his right side, finding his cigarettes, then the Zippo from a pocket of his Levis. He lit a Camel, the wind blowing hard and strong and cold, the smoke warm in his lungs, making him cough with the altitude. The altitude had been tiring him. Akbar was not tired; he was used to it.

Frost heard it the same time Akbar did, flattening himself against the rockshale wall of the ledge. Akbar

45

did the same, but his sword flashed out into a guard position as he moved.

Akbar looked at Frost, saying nothing. They both knew—Communists.

The one-eyed man swung the CAR-16 forward, but watched Akbar's eyes, moving side to side, then peering at the rifle. Frost nodded, slipping the rifle back along his side. Then he reached under his coat for the Gerber MkI. The blade flashed in the cold sun and Akbar's eyes lit, his head nodding approval. The Gerber looked like a letter opener in comparison to the long-bladed sword.

Akbar gestured for Frost to move back along the trail and Frost, keeping his back close to the wall, hearing the trickling of loose gravel as his pack brushed against it, started moving back. The Gerber was clenched tight in his right fist. Akbar reached under his coat with his left hand, the knife he carried there appearing in his left hand almost magically, wheeling in his fingers, the butt toward Frost. Frost nodded, shifting the smaller Gerber to his left hand, clenching the twelve-inch double-edged fighting knife that was Akbar's in his right fist now.

Akbar gestured with a palms-down signal, and Frost stopped, as did Akbar, but only for a moment. The fingers of Akbar's left hand started moving, as he counted to six. Frost nodded, judging by the voices and clinking of equipment that no more than half a dozen men were moving along the ledge. Akbar glanced behind him once, then started up a small ledge leading higher and away from the main trail, up a distance of perhaps seven feet. Then he moved laterally like a mountain goat down the length of the trail but from above. He gestured for Frost to stay put. Frost nodded.

It was Akbar's territory and Akbar's play, and so far the one-eyed man had seen nothing that injured his confidence in Akbar's abilities.

Frost flattened himself still more against the rocks, hearing footsteps now on the path, Soviet voices speaking words he could not comprehend. There was the unmistakable sound of a sling against a rifle barrel. The sound of one man tripping.

Frost glanced up once—Akbar was in motion, stripped of his pack, the sword held high in both hands, his body crouched like a cat's.

Frost tightened his grip on both of the knives, waiting, his palms sweating inside his double layer gloves.

"Amereekanski!"

The face was florid, shocked, the cheeks bleeding with cold from the tiny veins in the skin, the eyes blue— frightened suddenly as the Soviet soldier rounded the bend in the trail.

Frost rammed Akbar's long-bladed knife straight forward, into the Soviet soldier's neck. The one-eyed man then stepped away from the wall of rock behind him. Five more Russians were on the trail, their weapons coming up, a blur of gray and blue and flashing steel in the weak sun. The one-eyed man wrenched the knife from the neck of the dead man, slashing with the Gerber in his left hand. Then Frost brought up the large-bladed knife, the steel glinting red with blood. A Soviet corporal hauled up an AKM into an assault position, but suddenly the soldier's head tumbled from the shoulders, blood spurting up like a geyser. A whooshing sound was all Frost heard as he stepped in toward a third Soviet trooper, shoving aside the AKM's muzzle with his left knife hand, the knife biting deep into the soldier's right forearm. The knife in his left had hammered inward for the abdomen. Frost wheeled as the body fell, a hand sailing past him, the hand without a body.

He stepped back, Akbar finishing a cut with his sword, cleaving the head from a fourth man, then following through—hacking across the chest and down through the abdomen of a fifth man. This one had a bleeding stump where the right hand had been. Akbar wheeled. The one-eyed man dropped the knife from his right hand, switching the Gerber into that hand, underhanding it at the last Soviet soldier as the man raised his assault rifle. Frost's blade buried itself in the soldier's back in the same instant Akbar's dripping sword sliced into the man's neck. The man's head sheared away and began to tumble.

Frost couldn't help himself, staring at the head, listening to the dull thudding as it rolled down the side of the mountain beneath them, dropping, bouncing. Frost sidestepped as the body fell, catching it by the uniform tunic, then letting go, blood pouring down from the headless neck. The body flopped and spurted blood at his feet.

He looked at Akbar. There was no smile, but the determined look of survival.

Frost knew the look—it was on his own face, too.

Chapter Six

Frost ran low along the ridge, Akbar behind him rather than in front. The Soviet patrol—the six men they had killed its "outriders"—was below them less than a hundred yards, walking two abreast with weapons readied along the trail up into the Pass.

Frost glanced back to Akbar. Akbar nodded as he dropped to the rocks, the Springfield bolt action ramming forward and to his shoulder in a firing position. Frost turned, kept moving, his spot already picked, skidding down into it on his left thigh, the CAR-16 already swinging forward.

He ripped away the scope covers, ramming them on their elastic band into a side pocket of his peacoat, with his teeth pulling the leather glove from his right hand. The remaining rag wool glove was still there, protecting his flesh from the wind. He spread his legs wide, getting into a firing position as he extended the stock on the CAR, then put his eye to the scope. He adjusted his position and the rifle's for proper eye relief, settling the reticle on the Soviet officer commanding the patrol. Akbar would be sighted on him, too, so there would be no mistake.

Frost had the selector thumbed onto semi-auto as he squeezed the CAR-16's trigger, the reticle on the left ear, a little high for the neck shot he wanted. He finished the squeeze, the trigger's pressure gone, the rifle cracking once, bucking against his shoulder. His left ear rang as the .30-06 bolt action Akbar fired twenty yards away echoed across the rocks, the left side of the Soviet officer's face disintegrating under a wash of blood. The body rocked back—both Frost and Akbar had hit.

The officer fell, his men swarming toward him. Frost was already swinging the muzzle of the CAR onto other targets as he worked the selector by feel into the auto mode, then he began pumping the trigger. Three shot bursts hammered into the men surrounding their fallen officer. The booming of Akbar's bolt action echoed and echoing again, bodies to the rear of the patrol falling as Frost swung his own rifle there.

There was answering gunfire now, hammering into the rocks, the loud cracks of the thirty-caliber AKM slugs like tiny explosions. Rock chips and dust flew around the one-eyed man as he returned fire.

There had been twenty-four men, and as Frost changed sticks, hiding his head in the rocks, he mentally counted eight that he had killed or disabled, guessing Akbar to have gotten at least five from the number of shots expended. A fresh thirty-round magazine in his rifle, the rocks around him, powdering under gunfire, Frost rolled back, bumping over his pack, hoping he hadn't crushed the bottle of scotch wrapped inside four socks. Then he swung the rifle down again, on his belly now, firing indiscriminately into the men shooting up at him.

There was no shelter, not even concealment for the Soviet troopers below him. The Springfield was echoing again, bodies dropping. Frost pumped his assault rifle in a steady stream of three round bursts, men dropping.

He stopped shooting, as had Akbar. There was no answering fire from the trail below.

It was Akbar's voice as Frost stared downward at the bodies strewn about like discarded dolls. "You are American. It would offend you to do this. I will go and cut the throats of any who are still living."

Frost turned, standing now, staring after Akbar as—like a mountain goat—he almost floated over the rocks, his rifle slung on his back, his killing knife in his right fist.

Mechanically, Frost changed sticks in the CAR-16, holding it in a guard position toward the trail to kill anyone who might try for Akbar. There was no explanation for it, he thought. Except maybe he was getting soft. It was a war, after all.

Frost scratched at his stubbled face, sniffing, cold from the night spent in the rocks. His CAR-16, the magazines freshly reloaded for it, was held in an assault position as he followed Akbar Ali Husnain out of the narrow cleft of rock and onto the ledge. Below them, perhaps an hour's hard travel, was a village. "They will know we come," Akbar said matter-of-factly. "Food and fire are there—we will hurry," and he broke into a loping run.

Frost stared into the valley for an instant longer— trees, a fast-moving river or stream neatly bisecting the town, the town itself made predominantly of flat-roofed adobe-type brick houses and clefts cut into the rocks below them. The smoke from cook fires was visible, as were the vague shapes of what he imagined were children playing in the cold, windblown street. Dustdevils moving along that strut in the wake of cattle being driven there by amorphous, rag-draped men.

Frost slung the CAR-16 back, then broke into a run behind Akbar. Akbar was already a hundred yards ahead of him.

It was not a house, but a cave, a low tunnellike opening leading into it with a natural skylight formed by a chimney of rock above. After the middle of the day, it would be dark there, he knew; and the orange-yellow cook fire, aside from being the only source of warmth, would be the only source of light.

They had passed through the village to the mountains beyond. For the first time, Akbar had been wrong—it had taken an hour and a half to reach their destination, but inside himself the one-eyed man felt perhaps Akbar had slowed his run so as not to tire the American.

Frost leaned against the rock wall—gray like the clothes of the women who sat about the fire, their faces covered now with their veils as he had entered with the rest of the men. A prison they wore, he thought. Perhaps Margaret Jenks had been right about the Chadar. Frost's eye scanned the cave, seeing the faces of the men watching him, the humped shrouds of the women who watched him as well. But there was one face that was neither, nor was it the face of a child.

It was a woman's face, the eyes incredibly dark in the mixed glow of firelight and hazy sun. Her hair was shrouded in a black shawl, but her face from the high clear forehead to the determined and strong-looking chin was unveiled.

"Come—you see her, huh?"

Frost looked at Akbar. "I thought Moslem women here wore—"

"My wife wears the veil because she chooses to. This one does not—for the same reason. Merana. She is no man's wife and will never be maybe. She is a killer. She fights like three men, with rifle or blade. She is the last of her line. Three brothers and her father were killed fighting the Russians when they moved into Kabul in 1979. Her mother and two sisters were killed in a gas attack. She almost died—her lungs damaged. Even now she coughs much from it. She is a killer. That is all she is. She does not help the women, she does not offend the men—she is a non-person. She kills, that is all."

Frost studied the face. It studied him. "How old is she?"

"Sixteen, maybe—maybe not that much yet. But now we will rest here. The women make nan and there is meat. Come and eat and we will clean our guns and talk by the fire."

Akbar leaped once, down from the rock and onto the cave floor, Frost following him but not so gracefully. The eyes of Merana the killer didn't leave him.

Chapter Seven

He had eaten goat meat before and the women of the cave prepared it well, if anything overcooked. The one-eyed man wiped the grease from a stack of denuded goat ribs onto a rag and then turned to his pack, fishing out the Break-Free CLP in the plastic squeeze bottle and setting it on a rock away from the fire.

Akbar was unlimbering the two revolvers he wore. And Frost recognized them—.38-44 Heavy Duty Models, N-Frame Smith & Wessons dating from the mid-1930s. The grips were worn smooth of the checkering, the backstraps worn of their bluing—but aside from this and marks of holster wear, the guns were pristine; even the whited parts of the revolvers where the bluing was gone remained rust-free.

"You seem to do all right with whatever you use—but you wanna try some of this?" Frost asked, pointing Akbar at the Break-Free.

"I have seen this before. Yes—thank you, Captain."

Frost nodded, taking a piece of nan and then fishing into his pack for the bottle of scotch. "I know a lot of Moslems don't drink. Will this offend anyone?" Frost asked, peeling a white boot sock from the bottle, then another, then another, and finally the last one.

"No. Drink if you like. It clouds the senses though,"

said Akbar.

Frost shrugged, twisting off the cap and breaking the seals, then taking a pull from the bottle as he muttered, "Here's to sense-clouding, then."

They would sleep the night there and move out at dawn. Even though there were Mujahedin guards around the valley, Frost couldn't drink too much tonight. Akbar was right about that. He started cleaning his CAR-16 instead.

They walked in single file, Akbar well ahead with two of the Mujahedin leaders, Frost walking in front of the girl Merana. She looked smaller and younger. Her face was veiled now against the wind which lashed through the cleft in the mountains and blew ice spicules against their faces. Her eyes were like living things somehow independent of body or soul as Frost glanced back at her, forcing a smile. His own face was cold, his mustache stiff with condensed steam turned to ice. Her eyes said nothing to him.

He turned, facing the cleft of rock again, its knife-edged sides rising above them some hundred feet into the heavy gray sky, black patches in it of snow. The wind seemingly increased the deeper they penetrated the cleft. Frost shifted the weight of the assault rifle on his shoulder, digging his heels in slightly as they entered a spot where snow had already accumulated, his body cold, his lips dry but afraid to lick them lest the cold crack his flesh. He hunched his neck into the peacoat's collar and walked on. . . .

Akbar had called a halt and scouted ahead. Frost sat now with his pack like a windbreak, hunched behind it.

The sixteen-year-old Merana hunkered beside him, sharpening a fighting knife on a stone.

"Do you speak any English?" Frost asked her finally.

"I speak perfect English," she said, then continued sharpening her blade.

"I was told about your family. I'm sorry," Frost told her evenly.

"I have killed sixty-four Russians, thirteen of them with a knife. This does not count of course the ones who have died from bombs I have planted or land mines I have buried. I no longer kill because of my family, Captain Frost. I kill because they are Russians."

"What if the Russians were to give it all up and pull out—leave?"

"I have no right to a faith anymore. So what you would call a sin in my religion, in what once was my faith—it would be meaningless. I am damned. I will kill myself—perhaps with this knife. But the Russians will be here for a long time, I think."

Frost didn't know what to say, but instead fell silent, watching the loving strokes she gave the steel as she honed its edge.

Akbar soon returned. "One hundred and fifty Soviet troops—too many for us now. There are more Mujahedin where they travel and they will not escape justice. But we must pass around them. The snow falls heavily."

Frost looked at his half-covered boots and watched as the snow compressed into lines of crystalline ice in the wrinkles of his peacoat.

"If we wait for them, perhaps the snow will be too great and we shall die in it. We must get off the mountain. So we go around the Russians to find the Mujahedin of Babrak ul-Raq and the American Matt Jenks. You agree, Captain, to this?"

Frost let out a long sigh, watching the steam form in a cloud in front of him. The air was still as heavy snow dropped over them like feathers. "Yes—I agree, Akbar. The mission is to reach the Mujahedin who worked with Jenks and to learn of the Soviet weapon and save Matt Jenks. Not to fight the Russians."

"Each one we kill is one less," Merana said emotionlessly.

"And if we die," Frost said without looking at her, "and the Russians have some new type of weapon, perhaps many more will die."

"We will die anyway," she answered and Frost looked at her. She said nothing more.

"We go now," Akbar nodded solemnly. Frost stood up and shook the snow from his jacket, beating it from his pants. His feet still moved at least, but were stiffening. . . .

The girl, Merana, was in the lead as they started across the mountain face on the far side from the pass through which the Russian forces traveled. And watching her move, Frost could well understand why she had been chosen. The lightest in weight, now that the wind had heightened again, she faced the greatest danger of being swept off the ledge along which she moved. But the lightest, the one with the smallest feet, she also had the best chance of hammering in the knives that were used like pitons and supporting herself until the rope railing was laid. A shelf extended from the far side, then a high, narrow rock chimney Frost could see clearly as he waited beside Akbar and some of the others. Once they crossed the precipitous face of the mountain, they would climb up the chimney. Snow fell heavily and blew with lacerating intensity at Frost's face as he watched the girl and the rock chimney beyond. He could see snow from the higher elevation being blown down the chimney and hear it even as it whistled downward. It would be necessary to fight the rock surface, the force of gravity which would pull at a body to drag it from the meager purchase there might be, and the howling icy wind. The wind would abate for an instant, and Frost could see the rock face inside the chimney—it glistened with ice.

Frost shifted his gaze to the girl, Merana, now more than two-thirds of the way across the rock face, wind-born snow swirling about her, the clinking of metal against rock audible as she hammered another knife into the cracks. Would they hold more than a girl of perhaps ninety pounds? Frost wondered. Leading back from her body was another rope, the rope cinched about her waist, the other end held like a tether by Akbar. Should she fall, the rope would do her no good, Frost realized. She would be dead from the pendulum motion of the rope as it swung her against the rock face, if her back didn't break first. But it was this second rope on which their hopes of crossing the rock face with full gear depended.

Once across, this second rope would replace the use of the meager ledge across which she moved, the ledge being too small to risk getting a dozen men with full equipment over it.

She was driving in the last of the knives and Frost watched her as she leapt from the ledge and onto the shelf beneath the chimney, her footing going, her body twisting crazily, then knifing forward. Her hands reached out, catching at something as she recovered her balance. Frost thought he could detect a smile as she waved that she was all right.

"Turel!" One of the men near Akbar and Frost shouted the word.

Frost looked at Akbar. "Turel?"

"Bravery, Captain—it means bravery. Turel!" He shouted the last word across the rock face. The girl made as though she hadn't heard it, Frost never doubting that she had.

"Turel," the one-eyed man murmured.

Akbar had crossed, as had half of the others when Frost set his left foot onto the lower of the two ropes, his gloved hands clutching the ice-encrusted rope above him that was lashed across the rock face by the fighting knives used as pitons. Ice also coated the lower rope. Frost felt it as he shuffled his left foot outward, the rope just ahead of his heel in the hollow between heel and sole. He got his right foot onto the rope and started across, the going doubly slow. It would have been a precarious crossover under any circumstances, because the strength of the moorings for the handrope was dubious, and an expanse of fifty yards pressed against a rock face with only a single rope to support the feet was shaky. But with the driving wind and the ice on the ropes, it was that much worse.

He threw his weight forward, knowing his back would ache for it. But he had to get his center of gravity over the rope because of the backpack he wore and the rest of his equipment.

"Come, Captain," Akbar called. Frost glanced away from the rock face, licking his lips despite the cold and nodding. He made no bones of how he felt—terrified. He didn't look down. He had assessed the drop to a narrow ledge of rock below him as perhaps three hundred feet. And if the fall to the ledge didn't kill him, the likelihood of remaining on the ledge was slim, and the drop past the ledge was another five hundred feet into a rocky gorge.

He moved his left boot, then his right, feeling his footing slip where the ice was thicker, holding himself up with the guide rope against the rock face. Then he threw his weight again as he heard the terrifying sound of steel against stone. One of the knives securing the rope working its way out of the rocks.

The one-eyed man kept moving—fifteen yards remaining. Left foot, right foot, left foot—he felt himself slipping again, tucking up his right foot, leaning heavily against the rock face.

"Captain, lesta sha!"

"What?" Frost shouted over the wind.

"How are you—you are making it?"

Frost didn't waste his breath to answer, but merely nodded. He placed his right foot down firmly again— as firmly as possible—and moved on. Left foot, right foot—ten yards to go now, he gauged. Akbar was already reaching out to him, the girl crouched placidly beside him.

"Captain!"

"Coming," Frost shouted back.

Left foot, right foot, left foot, right foot. The right foot slipped on the ice, Frost dangling for an instant from the guide rope, more noise of metal scraping rock, a knife working loose. "Shit!" he murmured, looking down, seeing the ledge three hundred feet below, and the drop past the ledge. "Not getting me," he rasped, tugging on the guide rope, getting his right foot up, then his weight back against the rock surface. He kept moving, his fingers numb with the cold, his face beyond numbness. Left foot, right foot, left foot, right foot . . . A yard, Akbar's hands reaching out for him. Left foot—left foot again, the right foot, his left hand reaching out, grasping Akbar's right wrist. Akbar's gnarled fingers knotted across Frost's own wrist and into the forearm. Left foot, right foot . . .

"Now, Captain!"

Frost jumped, reaching for Akbar's left hand, his feet slipping slightly. Frost threw his weight forward, sinking to his knees on the ice-coated rock shelf.

"Some—some of the knives—working loose," Frost gasped, the wind cold in his lungs.

"I will fix them."

Frost looked up, the girl standing now and moving past him. She jumped out to the ropes, moving across them like a spider on a wall. Frost stood up, sinking against the wall of the rock chimney, a cold wash of snow showering him. But his breath was coming back to him as he squinted against the driving snow and watched Merana re-securing the knives along the length of the guide rope so the others could make the passage.

Frost's numbed fingers found his cigarettes and his lighter, and he pulled off the leather outer glove on his right hand to light a Camel, the Zippo shielded in his cupped hands. He let the cigarette hang in the left corner of his mouth, ramming his right hand under his left armpit to warm it. He stomped his feet to get feeling back into them, watching as the girl sprang back onto the rock shelf. She glanced at him once then shouted in one of the twenty Afghani languages Frost didn't know.

Another man started across the rope bridge.

Chapter Eight

Akbar had taken the lead, his strength more needed than Merana's sheer agility as one at a time they started up the chimney. The snow kept washing down in heavy gusts, driving at their faces. Akbar had given Frost a length of rag and now the one-eyed man more closely resembled his companions, he felt. Tied burnoose fashion as the others wore theirs, over his cap it served to warm his head. The "blessed" part of it, the one-eyed man felt, was the protection it gave his face, which it covered completely except across the bridge of his nose and his right eye.

There was Akbar first, then two of the others, then Frost. Behind him—perhaps because he had demonstrated little grace in his earlier climb, he thought—was Merana.

The chimney, as Frost started through it, was perhaps a yard wide, the rock face smooth. Akbar used the knives again as pitons to hammer into the surface and make purchases for himself as he moved up the chimney's height. Here, Frost realized, the girl was at a disadvantage. Her arms and legs were shorter and with each new set of blades she stretched her body to the limit.

Frost studied Akbar as the man disappeared suddenly in a bend of the chimney. Snow fell on Frost and the others ahead of him as Akbar's footing dislodged drifts caught in the bend of the chimney. Frost blinked the snow away, continuing upward, reaching with his left hand, then pulling up as he extended his right hand and right leg. He felt like a clumsy man climbing a too-large ladder.

There was a sound—not a scream but a rapid intake of breath—and Frost looked down, his right fist snaking out, balling into the shawl and the hair of the girl, her body slipping through the chimney, then hanging for a moment. Frost held her. Her hands shot out and she reached for the knife handles and pulled herself against the ice-coated wall.

She looked up at him quickly, pain in her face but not in her eyes as Frost unknotted his fingers from her hair and her shawl. She leaned heavily against the rock, with her left hand quickly rearranging the shawl across her waist-length black hair. Her eyes flickered up then, her mouth open as if to speak.

Frost looked at her and smiled. "You're welcome, kid," he told her, then started to continue up the chimney. He felt something tug at his pants leg and he looked down. "What?"

"Nothing," she answered, then looked away.

The one-eyed man only nodded, then continued the climb.

Moments later Frost shouldered his way through the last yard or so of the chimney's height and rolled onto the snow-covered rocks above, letting out a long sigh, watching the steam of his breath freeze.

Akbar clapped him on the shoulder. "You did well, Captain. We will make a mountain man of you yet."

"Sure," Frost nodded, edging back from the chimney for a moment, then reaching forward to the gloved hand reaching out. He grasped it at the wrist and pulled the girl to the surface. Her shawl and her shoulders were covered with snow, her eyes flickering as she surveyed the top of the mountain.

As he pulled her up, she shook herself of the snow, then shook her hand free of his, looking at him once. Then she shifted her AK-47 into an assault position and began running across the snow toward the edge of the flat expanse at the top of the mountain.

Frost helped Akbar pull the rest of the men up, the two who had followed Akbar already at the rim, the girl beside them now as Frost glanced back at her.

Frost got to his feet, brushing away snow, loosening the CAR-16's sling and shifting the weapon to an assault position. "Any more climbing—up or down?"

"No, Captain—not like this." Akbar smiled, adjusting the position of his sword across his back. "At least I do not plan any more," and again he clapped Frost on the shoulder. "What?" Akbar turned, Frost following him. Merana ran toward him.

"What is it, girl?"

"Soviet troops along the ridge. Perhaps fifty—the snow is so thick."

"Shit," Frost murmured.

"Yes—shit, indeed," Akbar nodded. "They cannot

find us here in the open."

"A sniper could slow them and allow the others to escape." She looked over her shoulder. "I am the best shot and the smallest target."

"I could do it better," Frost told her. "See, with one eye, I don't have to squint with a scope and—"

"You cannot. You and I must get out of these mountains and to the north with as many of these others as possible. She is right," said Akbar.

"No, dammit, Akbar. I'm not leaving—"

"A girl? I am a killer first." She ran off toward the rim, calling over her shoulder, "I will meet you at the village, Akbar!"

"No—" Frost started after her, feeling Akbar's hand on his shoulder. Frost wheeled around. "She'll—"

"She will not. And if she does that is what she wants. You cannot change her—you cannot change the people here." Frost heard the first shot from her scoped AK. "We go," Akbar said with an air of finality.

The one-eyed man felt his lips curl into a snarl, shot a glance at the girl. With the others he started running across the mountain top and toward the ridge line just barely distant at its far edge. . . .

Frost crouched in the rocks, peering down into the village. "The Russians have been here already," he murmured in little above a whisper, then turned away from the village and recapped his binoculars.

"We cannot go in yet. The gas," Akbar said through his teeth. "Another hour and perhaps it will be safe."

"I know," Frost answered, still hearing the cry of a child from the village below.

The cry lingered, coming less and less often over the next twenty minutes as Frost watched the Rolex's second hand sweep its course. And then the cry stopped completely and Frost knew that the child down there in the swirls of gray and red that hung close to the ground had died.

Chapter Nine

Frost looked up from his hands. It was warmer here in the shallow valley and his hands were not cold, but they were mud-stained from helping to bury the dead. There had been forty-one children's bodies. He had no way of knowing which one had been the crying child whose voice had haunted him while they had waited to enter the village.

At the edge of the village now, Akbar and some of the others were talking. He saw the men turn.

He stood up, looking beyond them. Running like an animal rather than a human, an even gate that seemed tireless, was Merana. Her scoped AK was held at high port in her tiny, gloved fists.

Frost shook his head, picking up the CAR-16 and his pack and then started toward them, shifting the KG-99 on his back.

"I saw them—the pigs—the pigs! I started shooting at them, at their decontamination vans, at all of them. They follow me now! We can kill them all!" The girl was screaming as she ran.

Frost dropped his pack. He wanted now to kill them all too.

*   *   *

There was a three-story, narrow stuccoed house beyond a line of ragged, denuded trees. Frost moved toward it. The Russians were four hours behind them, confined to roads rather than the mountain passes Frost and the others had taken with Akbar at the lead.

The gravel slipped under his feet as he started up the embankment toward the structure with its glassless windows, the grayness of it muted against the winter sky. But it was almost warm by comparison to the mountains they had traveled through in the night.

Frost scratched at his growth of beard, then glanced at his watch. It was nearly eleven A.M. and it spelled thirty hours without sleep. His eye burned with it, but after the bad period of grogginess he was alert enough.

There were thirteen men, counting himself, to face twenty times that number of Russians. The Russians came with heavy equipment as well. Frost shrugged, not caring. What had to be done had to be done. He reached the house finally, stopping in the doorway. The door was broken down, fire having partially gutted the house. He set his pack down outside—it was cleaner there—and walked inside, Akbar behind him.

The ceiling was splotched with gray light where the roof was gone in parts and Frost stared up at it. "A sniper here who can get out quick."

"Yes—a sniper here who can get out quickly. Yes," Akbar nodded, Frost looking at him.

"The land mines?"

"They are being planted along the roads in so obvious a way even the Russians will not miss them,

I think."

Frost only nodded, starting out of the house. He rested his rifle against his pack, the burnoose stripping away and his right glove following it. He searched his pockets for a pack of Camels, lit one, and stared at the white trunks of the trees beyond and below the house.

"The Russians will be coming soon," Akbar said, standing beside him suddenly.

"Maybe not just here if we don't watch out," Frost said quietly, exhaling hard. The wind was cold. . . .

Frost gathered that men and women prayed separately in the Moslem world, or at least Merana prayed separately. He wondered—perhaps she prayed for her death in battle. The men were on their knees, faces to the ground, facing to Mecca so far away, and a short distance from them knelt Merana, her rifle beside her. Frost stood in the gap of rocks overlooking the road beyond the destined battleground, taking the tour so the others could pray. At twenty-to-one, the odds were less than favorable for survival, however optimistic he could convince himself to feel. He did something he hadn't done in a long time—he made the sign of the cross. The sun remained cold and could not warm him. Mechanically he was checking his weapons and he looked up. In the far distance along the horizon he could see the faint outline of movement. He murmured something that he guessed was a prayer, then snatched up his CAR-16 and started to run toward the others. It was time now.

"Allah be with you," Akbar murmured.

"God be with you," Frost answered, the two men looking at each other and Frost feeling himself smile. He lay beside Akbar in the rocks above the trees separating the house from the lower ground, the house two hundred yards to his right. Merana, of course, was in the house—positioned as the sniper. Frost had not been at all surprised when she had volunteered, and Akbar admitted she was a better shot than even he.

Thoughts of the mission were gone, the more important matter being revenge against the Soviet troops for the gas attack, the dead children, the one Frost had heard crying as it died, the one he couldn't recognize from the rest as he had helped with the burying.

Trip wires interlaced the road, connected to explosive detonators which would trigger chain reactions in the wiring to the land mines buried there. Plastic explosives were packed against the trunks of some of the larger trees to fell them across the road and trap or at least slow the Soviet mechanized equipment. There were no tanks—the only vehicles being Soviet jeeps and their gas trucks and decontamination trucks.

The attack would have to be swift. Neither Frost nor any of the others had gas masks or protective clothing, and if the Soviets were able to use their gas they would win the day.

Frost watched. His body tensed, an involuntary chill—not from the cold—traversing his spine as the first of the Soviet troopers crossed the low rise, walking parallel to the road rather than on it.

"You will fire the first shot?" Akbur murmured.

"Yes," Frost answered him, settling the CAR-16's stock to his shoulder. He settled the Colt scope's reticle

71

on one of the mine-sweeping team, seeing the man's face clearly. Mine sweeper work was done by either the very young or the very old. The senior non-coms would know enough to feel a slight depression in the ground where the mine had settled before finishing a footfall. This face was very young, a blunted nose that slightly upturned, skin tinged cherry-red with the cold, ears that stuck out under the helmet. The young man's tunic was buttoned to the neck and the neck seemed to stand out from it, as though the tunic was many sizes too big. Perhaps he had lost weight, Frost thought. It happened in the military—a dramatic loss to ideal body weight or slightly below. Or perhaps Russian quartermasters were just as blind as American ones. The thought amused the one-eyed man for a moment as he held steady on the bridge of the young man's nose.

As the trail of the column became visible, Frost swung his scope away to more accurately gauge its composition—at least two hundred and fifty men, most walking, but some in canvas-topped trucks. There would be machine guns in the trucks. He eyed the gas vans. Two of Akbar's men had grenade launching devices fitted to their rifles and when Frost triggered the first shot, they would take aim at the gas trucks.

He would fire, they would fire, and Merana would open up her sniper fire on vehicle drivers and other targets. Six more of Akbar's men on the other side of the defile would open up with their automatic weapons, Frost and Akbar joining them in a crossfire. Akbar's Springfield was replaced for the time being with an AK-47.

The two men remaining from Akbar's force were

moving into position to the rear of the column. These men carried automatic weapons to be fired from moving positions and make it appear there were a larger number of men than there were. Textbook-wise, Frost thought. The plan had a prayer, however modest a one.

But reality would be another matter.

Frost resettled the scope on the bobbing Adam's apple of the Soviet soldier with the mine sweeper, seeing his eyes peering intently at the ground and at his machine. Frost touched his finger to the CAR-16's trigger, the selector already on semi-auto.

"Shoot," Akbar rasped.

"I will," Frost murmured not taking his eye from the scope. He watched the Soviet soldier's flickering eyes— he was little more than a boy. Deciding he was getting soft, Frost swept the scope to the next man in line, not studying the face, not looking at the eyes, not conjecturing what kind of human being lay behind them. He pulled the trigger. The man's neck erupted in red, the eyes wide open. A sudden drop to the jaw signaled death and then the body toppled to the ground.

Gunfire was all around him now and as Frost thumbed the selector to full auto and swept the assault rifle for a target, he saw two things—the first of the mines exploding and through the cloud of dust and rock chips and blood and specks of flesh he saw the young Russian soldier. Someone else had shot him, a gaping hole between the eyes that an instant before had flickered nervously.

Frost swallowed hard, picking up a target, firing, then sweeping the muzzle before the body fell, firing again in neat three-round bursts, splitting foreheads, severing jugular veins as the enemy fought back. The mines exploded in line now down the road. The different explosive cracks of the rifle grenades sounded as they aimed for the drivers' compartments of the gas trucks.

Drivers were slumping behind their steering wheels as Frost's scope passed them—the work of Merana from her sniper's nest.

A mortar crew was setting up. Frost changed sticks in the CAR-16, ramming the empty into his belt. The one-eyed man fired, hot brass pelting his left cheek and his exposed neck as Akbar's AK-47 roared deafeningly beside him.

"Up," Frost shouted, a mortar whooshing out of its tube. Frost started to run, shooting out the CAR-16. He swung it back on its sling empty, then pulled the KG-99 forward, the bolt already closed over a live round, the safety off. Holding the barrel in his left fist, the pistol grip in his right, he started pumping the trigger. Soviet soldiers ran out of the tree line and toward them, the mortar exploding less than fifty yards behind them. Frost wheeled for an instant. Merana should be coming out of her sniper's nest. As he stared at the partially demolished house, a mortar round arced toward it with a whistlelike scream. The house shuddered, then suddenly it began collapsing.

"Merana!" the one-eyed man snarled, chunks of the house bouncing up from the ground in a billowing cloud of dust.

Wheeling, he leveled the KG-99 from the hip into three Soviet troopers charging toward him, cutting them down with rapid semi-automatic bursts. Then he hit the ground, rolling, Akbar on his knees beside some rocks, firing his AK-47. Frost rolled into the rocks, running out the 36-round magazine for the KG-99, then ramming a fresh stick home. He worked the bolt, pumping out two three-round semi-auto bursts, cutting down still another of the Soviet soldiers.

He snatched at the CAR-16, replacing the spent magazine, then pushing to his feet. The CAR-16 belched flame from the shortened muzzle, two Soviet troopers going down.

"Come on!" Frost yelled to Akbar, racing down into the defile beyond the trees. Gunfire was heavy now from the far side where the six marksmen were. Frost aimed into the same target area as he paused in the trees, spraying the Soviet troopers below, the muzzle of his assault rifle bucking up, held in control by his aching arms. Then the rifle fired again, his ears splitting with the ringing of the explosions as more of the mines were set off. Trees fell across the road now, but one of the gas trucks was moving.

Frost ran forward twenty yards and dropped, ramming a fresh stick into the CAR-16, firing it into the windshield of the gas van. The glass shattered, the van lurching over the downed tree blocking its path. The van started to tip over, to roll, fire gushing from its gasoline tanks now as a rifle grenade blasted it.

Frost pushed himself to his feet, running now toward the killing ground. Akbar shouted to him, the AK-47 held high in his left fist over his head, the sword high in his right.

Frost slowed, bracing a pair of Soviet soldiers,

pumping rounds from the CAR-16 into their chests and abdomens and necks, the two bodies falling. The one-eyed man wheeled, a half dozen of the Soviet troopers pursuing him from the tree line. Frost slung the KG-99 around, firing it from his right hand. Then he reached under his coat, snatching awkwardly at the Metalifed High Power in the Cobra rig there, thumbing back the hammer. He triggered a two-round burst to his left, then both pistols in his hands, firing into the six, now five, now four, now three Soviet soldiers. The KG-99 empty, Frost shifted the pistol to his right hand, then buttoned out the magazine in the High Power. The magazine was nearly spent, and he rammed a twenty-round extension magazine from his belt up the well in the grip; then he continued to fire, the pistol in both hands.

The slide locked open, the one-eyed man crashing the pistol down across the face of a man rushing him. Frost wheeled, grabbing at Akbar's killing knife, his left fist wrapped around it, the knife ramming forward into the chest of a Soviet.

No time to retrieve the knife, Frost sidestepped a man coming at him, lashing out with his right foot as he wheeled. The toe of his combat boot hammered into the right side of the soldier, knocking him to the ground.

Frost finished the move, stepping into the man, his left foot kicking out. He pounded once, twice, three times against the side of the man's head, the helmet launching into the air like a football.

Frost spun around, ramming a fresh twenty-round magazine into the High Power, firing as soon as the slide closed, two rounds into the face of the Soviet soldier running toward him, the bullets impacting just under the lip of the helmet.

He saw Akbar, his sword flashing unnaturally in the gray light, a head spinning off a Soviet soldier, a cry on Akbar's lips, then an explosion. Frost fell forward, rolling with the impact, on his back now raising the muzzle of the High Power. A mortar crew from the far end of the road was shooting into the fighting. Frost rammed the High Power into his belt, shifting the CAR-16 into position, replacing the emptied magazine, running toward the mortar crew. There was a whooshing sound. Frost threw himself to the ground, rolling against an overturned gas van. The mortar exploded—arms, legs, indefinable parts of bodies and equipment sailing skyward. He was up again, running, firing short bursts from the CAR-16 as Soviet troops launched themselves toward him. The mortar crew was now twenty-five yards distant.

The closest man had his round, was dropping it down the tube. Frost fired, the body spilling over the tube as the mortar left his hand. The mortar, and all the men around it, exploded. Then there was a secondary explosion, ammo perhaps—an orange and black fireball searing upward. Frost pushed himself to his feet, blood and flesh raining down on him, then wheeled. A Soviet trooper charged toward him with fixed bayonet. There was a solitary shot—Frost could hear it above the rest, thinking it was perhaps the shot that would kill him. But the Soviet soldier paused in mid-stride, the left side of his head seeming to bulge outward, then rupture. As the body spun, Frost could see the entry wound beside the right ear.

He glanced to his left. Merana stood there, her sniper

rifle in hand.

Frost turned, his CAR-16 leveled, but there was no gunfire—only the crackling sound of flames from the trucks that burned near him, and the screams of the Soviet soldiers as their throats were slit.

Frost closed his eye for a moment and breathed.

Chapter Ten

Frost thought oddly of one thing as they trekked down from the range of seemingly endless mountains and through another of the innumerable passes. After the battle, he had stopped Merana as she'd started to slit the throat of a Soviet soldier. He had told her simply, "He's dead already, dammit," and for the first time he had realized that perhaps the girl—walking now in silence beside him—was insane.

He was running low on .223 for his CAR-16 and despite the fact all the magazines were loaded, he'd taken a second rifle—an AKM—from one of the dead Russians, with all the spare ammo and magazines he could carry.

The march had endured for seven hours. More Soviets would come when radio communications with the destroyed gas column could not be made—perhaps Soviet helicopters. Distance was now paramount.

Akbar dropped back in the line of march, stepping in beside Frost, the girl moving back. Akbar said, "You fight like one of us—like a Pathan."

"These men aren't Pathans," Frost told him, smiling.

"Ahh—they are Afghani. All Afghanis can fight well. But Pathans of the Afridi fight best of all. You should be Pathan."

"Thank you," Frost nodded.

"Two more hours, maybe a little less, and we will be at the village."

"How much farther to the place from which Jenks worked?"

"Four days—maybe five, but we will ride there. You know horses?"

"Not too well—it was sort of forced on me once," Frost laughed.* "But I can ride if I have to. It's better than walking, I guess."

"You have been quiet, Captain—why?"

"Nothing much to say," Frost told him.

"The battle—it makes you silent?"

"It only made me wonder if your war here would ever end. Some of those men we killed were probably men like us."

Akbar nodded thoughtfully. "I have considered this—but no man should be Communist. He should either change his beliefs or die. It is the only way."

Frost laughed. "Can't let 'em walk all over your country. But things can't stay the way they are."

"They will never win. Even if they placed a man every meter apart in the entire country, in every mountain—there would be an Afghani or a Pakistani like me behind him with a knife. That man would kill the soldier and they would be short one man and then another and another until they were no longer a meter apart and there would be warfare again. This is the way of it. It will not change."

"What do you know about Matt Jenks? We never talked much about him."

See, THEY CALL ME THE MERCENARY #13, Naked Blade, Naked Gun

"Ahh—I saw him once, beyond those mountains and the next. He fought well and his eyes always moved, searching for things. They were blue eyes, very blue and strange to look at here behind a burnoose."

"What about the weapon?"

"It is not gas. They have perhaps tried all the types of gas they have. I do not think they would use a biological agent here—it would cause them too much difficulty. And little grows here if it were designed to destroy plants or trees. I heard a village woman once who had lost all her family. She wailed in the night and she had lost her mind I think. But she spoke about fire from the ground and the fire consumed all and made it vanish. This fire had killed her husband and her four sons. Perhaps this is the weapon, though what she meant by such fire I do not know."

"Fire?" Frost rolled the word on his tongue. There were exotic weapons in laboratories in each of the great nations of the world. One was rumored to exist that used varying frequencies of sound waves and could make an entire army vomit on cue, or turn cowardly. If it really existed he didn't know. There were other things. But fire from the ground?

Perhaps the woman had been crazy. Frost had seen that happen before—he had seen it too often.

"Fire," he said again. Akbar said nothing as they marched on, the snow thick and heavy beneath their boots as they crossed a niche in the pass. Beyond it, he knew, would be another of these endless valleys.

Chapter Eleven

There had been a house on a small piece of sandy land set out into the boiling waters of the river and Frost, Akbar, Merana and the others had crossed over to it along the sandy spit and stepped inside. He was tired. He said to Akbar as he cleaned his weapons, the Pathan doing the same, "There should be guards. We're too vulnerable here."

"Merana will guard. They will soon come and ask that as a woman she have separate sleeping accommodation from ourselves. The house above ours is that of the village headman. I know him well—he would die before letting the Russians come for us."

"We set out tomorrow?"

"On horseback. It is like nothing you have ever experienced—the horses here are fast and they streak across the desert like the wind itself. They breathe fire sometimes," and Akbar laughed, clapping Frost on the shoulder with his gun-oiled hand. "There will be a feast tonight—pilao and fresh milk."

"Pilao?"

"It is mutton—with carrots and rice and sometimes raisins. It is good. And the milk will help you to fight the grease if your stomach does not like grease."

"Is that water in the stream potable—for a Western stomach?"

"It is clear, from the mountains. Very cold."

"Good. As soon as Merana leaves I'll bathe."

"Bathe?"

Frost only nodded, putting the bolt back in the CAR-16. . . .

There were worn rock steps cut there perhaps a hundred years ago—he didn't know, but he took them down, wearing only a shirt and pants and no socks. He was already cold without even touching the water, but determined. He crouched beside the swirling water, the house above him, a steel pocket mirror propped against a rock outcropping, a Gilette with a fresh blade in his right hand. He studied the beard on his face—too much gray there. He set down the razor, reaching into the water and splashing it across his face. It was icy cold.

He took his shaving mug and the brush, cupping water into the mug with his fingers and swirling the brush in it against the dried soap to make a lather. He worked at the lather for a time, so cold now he could barely feel it. Then finally he looked into the mirror again and spread the lather over his cheeks and chin and neck. He preferred an electric razor but doubted even had there been electricity that an electric razor could have tackled the weeks' growth he had. He set the brush in the mug and began chiseling at his face with the razor, seeing the skin of his face finally. He rinsed the razor clean of soap and hair in the stream.

He finished the shave, studying his face in the mirror. The scar which his patch usually covered was as it always was. He thought back to the loss of the eye—this, not the cold, made him shiver. He dried the razor blade on a towel and then looked about him toward the bank—but there was no one. If a Moslem woman saw him naked it could create problems, he knew. He stripped away his shirt and his Levis, then his underpants and stepped down into the water, the shock making him catch his breath. He let the water numb him before he raised himself from it to wash his body and his hair.

Wearing clean clothes, except for the British Army sweater and the combat boots—the smell from them was unpleasant if the wind were right—he stepped into the house. Merana and Akbar were talking. Then Akbar left, the others already gone. Merana looked at him.

"So that is what you look like, Captain Frost. You are a pleasing man."

"Thank you. But you're sixteen," he smiled, "so I'll forget you said it."

"I am washing the clothes for the men. So I will wash yours. Some of the women will help me. Give me your things—there—under your arm."

Frost looked at the Levis, surprised they couldn't stand up by themselves.

"You don't have to do that."

"I was born a woman. I do not live like one, but there are things I will do. This I will do for you, and for Akbar. Not because I am a woman but because it would be unseemly for you to perform such a task, and it is not for me. Now give me the clothes."

"How did you survive that building when the mortar hit it?" Frost asked her, handing over the garments. "I'm afraid they smell badly."

"We have strong soap."

Frost nodded, lighting a cigarette. He noticed her nose wrinkling up. "The smoke bothers you?"

"The boots. Sit down. I will take them off you."

"No—they're the only boots I have with me."

"Your feet will rot. I can fix them so they do not smell. Sit down."

Frost sat down on a rock ledge at the side wall, starting to untie the boots, but Merana had dropped on her knees beside his feet and pulled the laces from his hands.

"I can do—"

"I will do it," she said calmly. Frost leaned back then, closing his eye, sucking the smoke deeply into his lungs.

She was removing the socks as well and he looked down at her. "I will be back in a moment," and she pushed herself off her knees and ran from the house. He smoked through the cigarette, then took another and lit it. Merana returned after a few minutes with a low dish stacked on top of another identical dish. "I will wash your feet."

"I just washed my feet—you leave my feet alone."

"You are not a Moslem man. I do not have to obey you. Now I will wash your feet," and she was already starting to bathe his right foot. The foot felt oddly cool—not from the coolness of the water, but as if something were penetrating the skin.

"What the—"

"I do not know what you call it in English—if there is a name. It is like a balm. You do not speak our language and so I cannot explain it to you. It will heal the feet—that is all."

"All right," Frost nodded, much too tired to argue. "How'd you get out of that house?"

"I killed two of the mortar crewmen, and while they searched for a man to feed the tube, I slipped out through the back. A piece of debris hit my head. I woke up and joined the fighting."

Frost leaned toward her, starting to touch at the shawl covering her hair. She reached up and grabbed at his hand. "No—"

"You can wash my feet, I can look at your head. Where did it get hit?"

Her eyes flickered up at him, and she let the shawl fall to her shoulders. She gestured at a dark bruise by her left temple under a lock of black hair.

Frost moved the hair aside, studying the bruise for a moment. "If it had been a hard enough hit you could have died, you know."

"I would rather die in combat than be killed by a piece of debris."

"Why don't you go be a woman. You'd be good at it. You have gentle hands."

"There are no men of my family to kill the Russians—so I kill the Russians."

"There must be other women like that," Frost told her, stubbing out his cigarette on the masonry wall.

"But I am not like that. Give me the other foot," she ordered.

Frost gave her the other foot.

He slept throughout the rest of the afternoon and

when he awakened, his boots were beside his pallet, shined. As he picked them up they no longer had any trace of his own odor, but rather something that smelled like an herb tea.

"Merana," Akbar said, then closed his eyes again and rolled over.

"Merana," Frost nodded, still staring at his boots.

Chapter Twelve

"He is one hundred years old. The rifle is older than that. The horse only four or five and is very fast. But he will outrun us for the first part of the journey, though he will not move out of sight. There is no need to keep up with him," Akbar advised.

Frost looked at the man about whom Akbar spoke. "One hundred years old?"

"Yes—in a few years he will not be able to do this sort of thing, I fear," Akbar said soberly.

"In a few years," Frost nodded, lighting a cigarette.

"It is the air—no smoke. Clean air—" Akbar filled his chest, the buttons of his coat straining with it against the buttonholes. "The mountains are a good life for a man." Merana walked past, loaded with her sack of belongings and her rifle, a smile flickering across her lips at Frost. "And a good life for a woman, too. Come and talk, Captain."

Frost nodded, patting the horse by its neck and catching up his assault rifle. It would be green in the foothills outside the village in the spring and summer— Akbar had told him so. "What do you wish to speak of, Akbar?" Frost said finally, inhaling on his cigarette.

"Of the woman, Merana. She responds to you. More than she has to anyone since the death of her family. I have seen her, on and off, for two years. This is the first time she has been human with another person."

"She's sixteen—just feeling her juices rising, I guess," Frost smiled. "I'm old enough to be her father, Akbar."

"Hadji—the old one. He is one hundred years at least as I have said. He has a wife who is less than thirty years. They live well together. Do you have a wife?"

"No," Frost answered, shaking his head. "But a woman I live with—someday we will get married if she can still stand me. Her name is Bess—she's a pretty woman," and Frost gestured to his face, "here," and then to his heart, "and here also."

"You do not ever take other women?"

"Well—" Frost stubbed out his cigarette under his boot heel. The boots still did not smell and he had worn them all the previous night at the feast and throughout the early morning. "That's not the point. I've got a woman. Merana is too young for me—or for you. I'm Western and being here doesn't change that—she's too young. But she is very beautiful."

"If you do this thing with her sometime because you want to, I think I would look the other way. She needs life put into her. Perhaps you can put it into her." Akbar shrugged then and picked white flecks of paper from the lower lip at the left corner of his mouth, holding the cigarette and inspecting it, then replacing it there.

"I thought Moslems weren't too hot on smoking either," Frost asked suddenly. "You know, like drinking."

"To smoke is all right. And anyway—I am not a perfect Moslem. But you are not a perfect Christian, are you, Captain?" Akbar laughed and patted Frost on the back, then started toward the horses.

Frost closed his eye a moment and shook his head, then followed Akbar toward the horses.

He wasn't certain if Afghan horses were like Arabians or not, but all of the horses had large, broad foreheads and were tough to ride. Akbar and the others occasionally punched an animal in the neck or head to make it ride more easily. Frost decided he had enough trouble holding on let alone starting a fight with the animal he rode. It was big enough that it might win.

Hadji, the old man, set a pace that neither Frost nor the others attempted to keep, the man almost constantly a half mile ahead of them, an outrider in function but feeling his oats in spirit, Frost thought. Across Hadji's back was the classic Afghan rifle. The gun itself was exceedingly long, a flintlock as Frost had ascertained seeing it close earlier before the old man had raced ahead. He was a rider without peer among his tribe and perhaps among all Afghans, Akbar had indicated. The curve of the rifle's stock made a gentle S-shape, the tail of the S lower than the height of the receiver by considerable distance, ornate beading and gold work on the wooden surfaces, and the rifle barrel itself a lustrous blue. A bit too lustrous to be genuine, Frost had thought.

Incongruously, the rifle wore a webbed sling, looking for all the world like something off an M1 Garand. And perhaps it was, the one-eyed man reflected.

Realizing he was falling behind, Frost put his knees to the horse, the animal rearing slightly and turning its head, nipping near his right foot. Frost dug in his heels and the horse started ahead. The one-eyed man would always like cars better, he thought.

Soon they were stopped on what in the American West Frost would have called a plateau—he was sure there was an Afghan term for it, because there seemed an Afghan term for everything else. He found that the languages were seemingly used interchangeably—Persian with something else, or something else with something else all together. He handed the reins of his horse to one of Akbar's men and started across the plateau on foot to stand behind Akbar and old Hadji. Merana stood some distance back, Frost guessed because of the age of the old man. He would likely disapprove of a liberated woman such as Merana. She smiled again as Frost neared her. The one-eyed man smiled back as he stopped beside her.

"What are they talking about?" Frost asked, not feeling rude for the question.

"They speak of the Buz Kashi—and how Hadji at one time won in a great Buz Kashi, the greatest of them all."

"Buzz what?"

"Buz Kashi, the dragging of the goat."

"The what—wait—I read about that. A race on horseback with the body of a dead goat."

"Yes, but since the Russians have come there is no time to play. I never saw one but stories were told of them by the other women of my village. Knives and chains were outlawed some time ago in the Buz Kashi. They thought, some of the government officials perhaps, that it was barbaric—to beat each other with chains and cut each other with knives to steal a dead

91

goat from another man and then ride away with it. There would sometimes be hundreds who would fight over the same animal. Hadji was perhaps the greatest of them—and he is the only one still alive who has been in so many of the events. He is a famous man, like you might have in your country with one of your games."

"Sort of like a pro football player," Frost nodded, then he laughed. "I can see that—the pro teams stealing away the football by beating each other with chains. Might make for an interesting game—hell on the uniforms though."

"Football?"

"Two groups of guys have a ball—"

"To whom does the ball belong?"

"What?"

"To whom does the ball belong?"

"It doesn't really matter. But they try to get control of the ball and run with it to make a touchdown."

"They cannot touch down without a ball?"

"No."

"Then why do not the ones who had the ball to begin with fight more hard so the other players cannot steal the ball and run away with it?"

"Well, they do. That's the idea."

"How do they fight?"

"Well—they knock each other down sometimes."

"What do they do then—after they knock down their opponent?"

"Sometimes they help them get back up to their feet, you know."

"This sounds like a crazy game," Merana said. "They let the men steal their ball, then pursue them and knock them down and then help them to their feet again so they can try once more to steal the ball. And no one really cares who owns the ball."

"Well," Frost began lamely.

"Buz Kashi is a much better game. What can you do with the ball anyway after you have it?"

"What?"

"The ball—can it be eaten?"

"No, of course not."

"A crazy game, as I have said."

Frost lit a cigarette and looked at her. "You're puttin' me on, right?"

"Putting you on right?"

Frost shook his head. "Never mind, kid—never mind."

Akbar turned around then, saying in English, "Captain, come here please and we shall see our next days' course."

"Good," Frost nodded. Merana was already turning away as Frost approached the edge of the plateau.

Beneath him, beyond a string of low foothills and wide cuts was a valley that could easily have been from some alien landscape. It was barren, rocky, split in long, winding cracks, and the cracks were filled with water. What might perhaps have been a road lay on the far side of the largest crack, white clouds on the horizon in the far distance, the sky blue and imparting a blueness to the water.

"It's beautiful," Frost said to Akbar.

"Maybe now you can see why we fight as we do. There is a rawness to this land that is life itself I think," Akbar said quietly.

The old man said something, Frost not understanding.

Akbar translated. "He rode here as a boy. He has ridden here many times since."

Frost patted the older man on the back, nodding as he pointed to the land below them, the old man smiling.

The old man started back to his horse then, his antique rifle slung across his back.

"You have a word in English—timeless," Akbar almost whispered. "That," and he pointed at the old man, "is the way we say it."

Frost only looked after the old man.

Chapter Thirteen

They rode down the slope, the old man for once riding slowly. The wind whipped at his coat and his burnoose, at the mane of the animal he rode, Frost staring at him. It was in some ways an idyllic life, he decided, then glanced at Merana. Merana looked at him, smiling like the girl she was and turning her face away, pulling the shawl more closely across it.

Frost looked back to his mount, feeling suddenly good aboard the animal. The water-filled cracks of lunarlike landscape stretched ahead of him, and beyond that was a cold and rocky desert.

The old man stopped, reining in his mount, looking skyward. He pointed animatedly. Frost looked skyward then, too, seeing nothing. Then he detected what might have been a speck on the horizon to their left.

The old man shouted something.

Akbar shouted the translation, the old man already taking off at a gallop: "A Soviet helicopter! We ride!"

Frost stared back at the speck on the horizon—he could barely make it out as more than a speck, and he heard nothing, but he dug his heels into his mount. Merana passed him, lashing out with her hand to his own mount's rump, the animal seeming to fly under him now. Frost bent low across the horse's neck, the mane lashing at his face in the wind, the animal's breathing something he could feel between his legs through the thin leather of the saddle. Froth blew from the animal's mouth, tiny droplets of moisture on the cool, dry wind.

Frost looked to the horizon again, daring to take his eye off the ground ahead of him and the horse under him. It was perhaps a helicopter, though he could hear nothing over the wind of the slipstream around him and the thudding, the hammering of his horse's hooves. He dug in his heels again, the animal seeming to quicken its pace.

The one-eyed man could see Hadji in the far lead, his rifle unlimbering like Frost imagined an Apache warrior of a century ago would have unlimbered his bow. And not far behind him rode Akbar, one of the two .38-44 Heavy Duty Smith N-Frames in his right fist. Merana unholstered a pistol as well—it looked like a Browning High Power from the distance, though Frost had never seen it before.

Frost carried the CAR-16 across his back, muzzle down and chamber empty; and, despite the pistol grip, with the added weight of the scope it wasn't ideally suited to one-handed operation. The liberated AK was strapped to his saddle, and no better suited to one-handed use. He swung the Interdynamics KG-99 forward on its sling, working the bolt and chambering a round, then shifting the sling off his body awkwardly with one hand. He hooked his left wrist into the sling, winding the sling there, his left fist balling around the pistol grip. He raked the shrouded barrel across the animal's rump to spur it onward, then held the 9mm assault pistol in his fist away from the animal, glancing toward the horizon again. It was a lone helicopter. But there would be a radio and more helicopters or ground forces would be called.

They were riding down into the flatlands, Hadji leading the way, his rifle at full extension skyward across his body—as if to let the Russian piloting the chopper know that the invader might win but he might be stung as well.

The helicopter was closing fast. Frost saw it clearly now as he looked up. It was a small craft and not a military gunship, but it would be armed. It skimmed the surface of one of the larger cracks, the water there showering upward like ocean spray against the rock face, the helicopter's right side open, a man leaning out of it. There was a glint of sunlight off the object the man held in his hands—a scope on an assault rifle, Frost guessed.

The helicopter was still a hundred yards off at least, but closing fast. For some reason—as though something told him to—the one-eyed man glanced ahead toward Hadji. The old man had both hands on his ornate flintlock now, guiding the racing animal beneath him with his knees alone.

There was a quick flash and a belch of gray-white smoke billowing on the slipstream. The helicopter's bubble dome took a hit, the helicopter rising quickly; and over the roar of the rotor blades and the wind, over the hammering of the horse's hooves, Frost could hear a wild shout. Hadji was riding the greatest Buz Kashi of his life!

Frost shouted as well, "Go to hell you Commie bastards!" He dug in his heels, his animal low over the ground now as he caught a glimpse of the shadow they

97

made in the sand. It almost seeming that there was an instant when none of the animal's four feet touched the ground. Flying, the one-eyed man raised the KG-99 in his left fist at full extension. The helicopter zoomed back now, the wind bringing Frost the lingering rotten-eggs odor of Hadji's black powder.

The one-eyed man began firing, the KG-99 bucking in his fist as he lowered his profile over the animal under him. More gunfire—Merana and Akbar and some of the others began shooting at the chopper. The chopper fired back, a steady stream of long automatic bursts, the sand kicking up around the riders. There was the shrill whicker of a horse going down— Merana's. Frost tugged at his reins, trying to head toward her before he passed her; but Hadji was already coming, the rifle slung across his back, his body hanging low off the right side of the saddle.

The old man's right arm scooped out like a hook, Merana on her feet, her bundle of possessions across her back with her rifle, a pistol in her right hand. Hadji swung even lower as the horse closed on her, and in the next instant she was up and across his saddle—like the goat, Frost smiled. "Like the damn goat!"

Hadji's mount reined in, reared, turned and sprang forward again. Frost was even with him now, the girl lying across his saddle and the horse's neck, the pistol in both her hands, firing skyward. Frost reined back to give her shot clearance, aiming his KG-99 as best he could toward the chopper's center of mass, the bubble itself. The Soviet machine was making a long, low pass, skimming over one of the cracks, water spraying now against Frost as the helicopter passed almost directly over him. Frost followed it, his left fist clenched tightly on the KG-99, the pistol bucking, the flat burping sounds of the 9mm 115-grain JHPs echoing on the wind. The helicopter suddenly rose.

Frost glanced to his right. Hadji was finishing reloading his weapon, again guiding the horse with his knees. Merana's shawl and her face were covered with lather spray from the horse's neck. Hadji now raised the rifle.

The helicopter was making a straight pass, the assault rifle blazing. Frost raised the KG-99, counting the stick as almost empty. In the same instant he fired, hearing Hadji's rifle boom.

There was a hit—the Soviet helicopter seemed to hesitate in mid-air, then started down with a roaring sound. The helicopter drowned the noise of the animals and the cries of Akbar's men. Then, suddenly, the craft erupted in billowing flames, orange and black and tinged with yellow.

Frost bent over his mount, the animal seeming to fly ahead as the wreckage of the chopper rained down on them, hot metal and fabric fragments falling against Frost's hands, the animal shuddering under him.

Akbar, ahead of them, was reining in. Frost now fought at his mount, the animal stopping so suddenly Frost almost pitched off into the sand—but he kept astride. And Hadji was beside him now, his mount skidding on its haunches in the sand, the girl Merana springing to the ground.

Frost looked at the old man. He said, feeling himself smile, "Merana, tell Hadji, the Buz Kashi rider, that the shot was his which brought down the helicopter. My assault pistol missed. He is the greatest rider."

Merana smiled—the warmest smile Frost had ever

seen cross her lips. She looked up at the old man in the saddle, and as she spoke the old man turned to face him, smiling, nodding, then giving his rifle a resounding pat.

Frost looked down to his own right hand, still clutching the reins, his fingers purple and stiff.

Chapter Fourteen

They had kept to the mountains for three days, hiding at times for hours in caves there with their horses. Soviet helicopters seemed to fill the skies, looking for them. But the searching had stopped and now they rode down through a narrow defile of marble smooth rock, a village sprawling before them. The houses were bleached by sunlight and bricks worn smooth by wind, terraced into the foothills. Children were playing in the streets, and armed men stood everywhere.

Dark eyes glanced upward at him as he rode; once or twice Merana, who rode beside him on the horse of the one dead member of Akbar's band, shouted down to the men and received an even angrier look in return. Frost didn't ask what she said.

Akbar and Hadji rode together at the head of the column, Frost and Merana behind them. Akbar turned his mount down a narrow dirt street and reined in before a house more worn and old-looking than the rest, but massive in size by comparison. Akbar swung down from the saddle, and as he walked toward the door of the house Frost observed the man's legs still seemed bowed from the ride.

"The village headman—a friend of Akbar's and of my father once," Merana told Frost. The one-eyed man merely nodded.

The door of the house opened and a man wearing the white turban of a mullah—a holy man—stood in the door. Akbar and the holy man spoke for some time, Frost squirming in his saddle, his rear end hurting.

"The holy man tells Akbar that Subhan and his force of Mujahedin are in the hills beyond the village—perhaps an hour's ride. The holy man suggests that Akbar and his warriors rest here, but Akbar declines. This is because of me. Akbar knows the holy man would not really wish to have a woman who dressed in men's pants and did not wear the veil to enter his home. So Akbar declines out of respect to the holy man."

"An hour's ride, huh?" Frost said to her, smiling. "I guess you're worth it."

She smiled and said nothing.

The ride was closer to two hours as Frost checked the Rolex on his wrist, dismounting the lathered and quivering horse. The animal, like he himself, was tired of the ride.

Akbar walked back from the man to whom he had spoken as soon as they had entered the Mujahedin mountain camp. He patted Frost's horse on the neck as he said, "Subhan is away—with a half dozen of his fighters—but he should return tonight. It seems that he too had been searching for Matt Jenks. We will sleep now. Their people will care for our horses, and we are as safe here as in a mosque."

"We have a similar expression," Frost nodded. "Safe as in a church."

"Here there are only Russians in great strength some ten miles away—but they do not know of the existence of this camp—yet."

"Safe as church, huh," Frost smiled, feeling his right eyebrow cocking upward.

"As safe as we can be anywhere here. We will all sleep." Akbar turned to Merana. "There is a place for you in our hut—Subhan knows of your work and there will be no problems."

The girl nodded, then started to lead her horse away. . . .

Frost lay on his back, listening to the girl breathing beside him. She had fallen asleep instantly, choosing to sleep between Frost and Akbar rather than near any of the others. She rolled over, her lips moving as though speaking as he turned to look at her. But no words came. Her right hand stabbed out in the yellow-tinged light of the low-burning fire, the hand moving frantically as though she were dreaming. Frost reached out and took the hand in his, the girl rolling closer to him, with both hands now clutching his hand. The movement of her lips stopped and her eyelids ceased to flutter.

Frost closed his eye, sleep coming to him, but not moving his left hand. . . .

He opened his eye, the girl arousing him. "Hank, you must come quickly. Subhan has returned and wishes to see you. Akbar is already with him."

Frost shook his head, trying to clear it. "What— Subhan?"

"He is back—with word perhaps of Matt Jenks, your friend."

103

"Matt—yeah," Frost nodded, sitting up. His left arm was slightly stiff.

The girl took his hand. She raised the hand to her lips, touching her lips to his fingers one at a time. "Thank you. A friend is something I never possessed," she murmured, then was up, running from the hut, Frost staring after her.

The tent of Subhan was larger than the others, torches lit outside it in the darkness, the black smoke rising on the wind from the torches toward the shelf of rock extending high above it. Frost wasn't certain of tent etiquette, so he knocked on one of the support poles, the two guards standing behind him, before he entered.

He pushed back the flap, walking through, seeing Akbar, the man grinning broadly for an instant as he saw Frost. Then Akbar said, "Captain, come in please and join us."

Frost nodded, then moved across the tent, warming now from the heat trapped inside it with only his British Army sweater on rather than his coat. It had been cold outside as he had approached the tent. He squatted on a red-patterned Oriental rug, beside Akbar. The man Frost supposed to be Subhan was on Akbar's right. Frost shifted his shoulders under his holster with the Browning in it and fished in his pockets for his cigarettes and his lighter, setting both on the carpet before his crossed legs.

"Captain Frost, Akbar has told me much of you. Welcome."

"Thank you," Frost nodded. "You are Subhan—and Akbar has spoken greatly of you and your—" Frost searched for the word. "Turel—your bravery."

"Ahh," Subhan nodded, his face breaking into a smile.

"I am told you know something of Matt Jenks—a friend to us both," Frost began.

"Yes—Matt Jenks—like you, American. A soldier. He has been missing for thirty-nine days from this camp. Each day he would go out with the same five men and not return perhaps for a week or better, always seeking to know of this new weapon of the Soviet invaders."

"And what do you know of this new weapon?" Frost asked.

"It breathes fire—but a fire that does not consume until it touches the target."

"You mean it's some kind of flame thrower?" Frost asked.

Akbar interrupted. "We have been all through this, Captain. He does not have the English words to describe it to you. But from what he told me—it is some sort of beam of light which burns its targets instantly to ashes if they are small. If it is a target like a vehicle, there is some burning and then the explosion. I have never heard of such a weapon."

Frost lit a cigarette, trying to make his hands calm. "Subhan—you have seen this weapon?"

"Many times. This is the weapon for which Jenks looked."

"I know what it is—what it has to be." Frost inhaled the smoke deep into his lungs.

"What is it, Captain?" Akbar asked finally.

"The Russians must have found a way of developing

some kind of sustained power source."

"What?"

"Akbar," Frost murmured through his smoke. "It's a laser. Not a targeting laser—we have those, I think. But a laser weapon." Frost shook his head, saying to both men, "Welcome to the future of warfare."

Chapter Fifteen

It had dawned cold. Frost and the others were already moving before the sun had come up between the mountain peaks; its orange light made long shadows for their horses as they clung to the mountain passes enroute to the Soviet base. After eight miles of the ten-mile trek, they had dismounted, leaving several of the men with the horses. Frost, Akbar, Subhan, one of his lieutenants, and Merana moved away from the others. Hadji had already set out in return to his village, leaving before dawn as had they. Frost clasping the old man's hand, the old man letting Frost shoulder his rifle. Merana had told him afterward that the old man never did this—it was a great honor.

Frost thought of it as they climbed what Subhan had said was the last of the small peaks before they could overlook the Soviet base on the plateau beyond. He thought of the old man, of Merana—of everything he could think of to prevent speculation over the Soviet weapon. He wanted to see it, to see that his assessment was wrong. He knew a great deal about guns, but little about science. He was probably wrong—maybe it was some kind of super-powerful flame thrower. But he thought back to the words in Matt Jenks' last dispatch—about bringing Western armies to their knees. A functional laser weapon that could be reused—as Subhan afterward had indicated this could be—shot after shot could bring the West to its knees in battle.

The thought sobered him. Frost realized that if such a weapon existed, the only chance for the West would be if he stole it. There would be more—but with a working model, even a prototype, American scientists could duplicate it. And perhaps then the Russians wouldn't use it.

They stopped at the height of the mountain, Frost moving to the front of the column, his binoculars already out. Merana and Akbar beside him, he belly-crawled across the few yards separating them from the edge, to avoid profiling himself and being seen from below. He stopped at the edge and peered over, focusing the right tube of the armored 8X30s, then looking down onto the plateau.

A fortress lay below, on three sides barren plateau across which movement of the smallest object could be seen for hundreds of yards. The fourth wall of the rectangular compound was against a drop.

"What lies below the plateau—on the far side?" Frost asked no one in particular.

He recognized Subhan's voice, answering. "It is impossible—a climb of some six-hundred feet—almost straight up. There are fewer guards there, yes." Frost could see that as he scanned the far end of the walled compound. "But the climb cannot be made, Captain Frost."

"I can make it," Merana murmured.

"Woman, no man can make this—you cannot climb this either."

The one-eyed man took the sixteen-year-old girl's face in his hands, her smile something any man would have called beautiful, he thought. There was nothing he could say. He kissed her lips, lightly, then hugged her to him, finding himself rocking her in his arms. Her arms were tight around him as though she would never let go. They sat that way for a long time, and then Frost got up, hearing the scratching sound of the oil can she carried for her guns being opened as he left the tent.

They rode through the night, the sound of the horses' hooves silenced on the rock by the snow which had fallen and continued now to fall. Frost once more wore the burnoose over his head to protect his face. His beard and mustache still were crusted with ice from the condensation of his breath. The horses too exhaled long shafts of steam as they breathed, their bodies trembling. The ride to the base of the mountain behind the plateau and the Soviet fortress above was a longer one, by another five miles. After the first ten miles they had stopped, dismounted and rubbed down the animals. There were thirty-five "volunteers," all but twelve of them from Subhan's band.

They rode on again for another four miles, leaving two of the thirty-five back with the horses and extra gear, then moving the last mile through the snow on foot. Frost felt the strain—in his legs, his back—as he waded through thigh-deep drifts. But he hardly dared to make a stray sound because there would likely be Soviet guards near the base of the cliff.

Akbar signaled a halt, Frost and the girl joining

Akbar and Subhan near the edge of a rock cleft. A hundred yards beyond was the base of the cliff, and near it a chainlink-fenced area, a perfect square. Inside it was a guard house, light shining from it. Outside of the guard house were two men. Frost watched in silence for ten minutes, seeing no signs of additional men in the snowy cold. He smudged snow from the face of his Rolex with his gloved right hand, then said to Akbar. "If we wait for a guard change I don't see any benefit for us—the time loss could be critical."

"I agree—yes. If we take the guards there will be no problem with communications. I speak perfect Russian and can fool them a little I think."

"Is there any language you don't speak?" Frost asked good-naturedly.

"My German is bad—very bad. How do we do this? Plaskewicz told me you are a mercenary, a commando."

"Three of us only, I think. Maybe six men there—two apiece isn't bad. You and me and one other—"

"I will go," Merana volunteered.

"And what if you're injured and can't make the climb?" Frost asked her.

"I will not be injured. I am silent—and good with this." She revealed her knife, drawing it from the sheath. "As good as I am with a gun—as good as you are."

Frost looked at Akbar, who nodded solemnly after a moment. "She is better than you with a knife, Captain."

Frost threw up his hands, saying nothing. He turned back to stare past the edge of the rock cleft. The

112

approach to the guard house was not a good one, but the best he could see on short notice. The fence would likely be electrified, but after taking out the two guards outside, it would be no problem to go through the gates to get the ones in the small house. Frost mechanically watched the smoke rising from the chimney of the guard house. He was very cold.

The biting wind had carved a furrowed drift away from the base of the cliff as it blew downward, and Frost, Merana, and Akbar had belly-crawled the hundred yards to the cliff face behind the cover of the drift. Frost's rifle had been left behind, the KG-99's muzzle covered with a dirty boot sock to keep it free of snow that might clog the bore.

He flattened himself now against the rock face, staring up along it toward the top which was obscured by snow and darkness. He shivered—not with the cold but with the thought of Merana scaling the cliff face. Before she would be half way up, she would be lost to sight.

He edged forward, Akbar and Merana behind him. Frost glanced back at her once, wondering how she did it without her teeth chattering and losing the knife—it was clenched there, edge out, ready.

The one-eyed man slipped the sock from the muzzle of the KG-99 and stuffed it into his pocket, pulling the folds of his burnoose closer around his face against the cold. Fifty yards remained until they reached the fence perimeter, then a crawl toward the nearest guard. Frost or Merana would get this man, Akbar then reach out with his sword for the fartnest man, the sword itself enough to confuse the guard long enough to kill him silently.

After twenty yards Frost made a palms-down signal, dropping into the snow and starting forward. He kept the KG-99 high out of the snow, his elbows shuffling him forward as his feet pushed him ahead toward the fence perimeter.

He could see the nearest guard, shivering, stomping his feet on the hardpacked snow of the path he had walked ever since Frost and the others had first seen him.

The man stood about six feet and was heavily built. A thin man would have died from lack of insulation tonight, Frost told himself. His teeth clenched, Frost kept going forward, stopping ten yards from the guard, hunkering down in the snow and reaching under his coat for his Gerber.

Like Merana, he put the knife in his teeth, but not so far back because it was double-edged and he'd seen more than one cocky man in combat fall and cut his mouth badly. The one-eyed man bit down hard, the steel still warm from being against his flesh. He slung the KG-99 across his back, then pushed himself up to his feet. He started running, in a low crouch, toward the nearest guard. He cut the distance to five yards, then four, his right hand reaching up and grabbing the Gerber, the knife in his right fist held tightly like a duelist would hold it, reaching to penetrate a kidney as he closed the distance. Two yards. The guard started turning. Frost threw himself forward, crashing against the guard and his rifle. Frost and the Soviet fell back into the snow.

There was a dark blur as Frost imagined Akbar jumping over his own and the Soviet's body. The one-eyed man rolled in the snow, trying to punch in his knife.

The Soviet's head snapped back, blood spurting across Frost's face and the burnoose. Merana's killing knife slit the man's throat.

Frost nodded to her, pushing the body away, getting to his feet. Akbar recovered his swing, a head rolling in the snow, a bright red swatch behind it, red speckles visible on the white snow in the glow of yellow light from the guard house windows.

Frost brushed the snow from the KG-99 as he started toward the gates, Merana beside him. There was a pad-lock on the gates. Frost turned to Akbar who held out a ring of keys, smiling.

Frost nodded, taking the ring, finding a likely looking key. The knife was back between his teeth, but cold now from the snow. He tried the key. The lock fell open. That was a good sign, Frost thought.

The one-eyed man looked at Merana and then at Akbar. There would be at least four men inside. Frost stepped through, the KG-99 hanging at his right side from its sling, taking his knife into his right fist. Akbar held his sword, the killing knife in his teeth. A little ahead of Frost was Merana, her long-bladed knife held in both tiny hands, poised across her right shoulder as she advanced.

Frost put the knife back in his teeth for an instant, removing his right glove, his moist hand suddenly freezing cold as he retook the knife.

He stopped at the door of the guardhouse. Merana was already under one of the windows.

She peered up and through, then ducked, holding up the fingers of her right hand one after the other—five. Then the thumb and the first two fingers again—eight men. The guard shifts would be short in weather like this, he thought.

Frost nodded, taking a deep breath, trying to focus his energy into his right fist and the knife he held there.

Merana stood ready with her knife, Akbar with his sword. Frost stood between them, taking a half step back from the door, then raising his left foot and snapping it forward as he swiveled. The impact against the door almost threw him off balance. The sound of the door shattering echoed loudly in the snow.

He finished the turn, his knife in his fist as he charged the shaft of yellow light from beyond the bizarrely hanging door.

Merana was already inside, and as Frost hit the room, he saw her lashing out with her knife, throwing her body into it as it made the arc. The tip of her curved blade caught the throat of the man directly in front of her, a gusher of blood spouting from the wound as she finished the turn and stepped into another attack. Frost was already moving, his knife digging deeply into the abdomen of the guard nearest him, his left hand pushing the man off, against another guard. Frost sidestepped, ramming the blade into the chest of still another man, then going for the soldier who was now crawling from under the body of the first man he'd killed in the guard house. He caught a blur of an arm or leg sailing through the guardroom air and bouncing against the far wall, a hideous scream of pain following it. Frost stepped into the third man, lashing his knife across the man's throat, then wheeling, Merana and Akbar together finishing the last man. Chunks of bodies littered the floor around Akbar's feet.

The one-eyed man bent to wipe clean his knife blade on an already-bloodied sheet. As he did, the head of the body in the cot fell and rolled across the floor.

Chapter Seventeen

There had been, so far, no ringing of the radio telephone unit in the guard house.

Frost and Subhan stood vigil at the base of the cliff. Akbar stayed inside waiting beside the radio telephone set lest it should ring. He hoped that his Russian could somehow convince the caller all was well.

Merana had disappeared from sight in the swirling snow and darkness up the cliff face more than twenty minutes ago. Frost checked the Rolex, smudging snowflakes from the crystal to do so.

"Subhan, how long would you estimate it should take for her to reach the top?"

"Perhaps another hour—if she reaches the top at all. It is smooth rock—she carries heavy equipment in order to make the climb. There is ice and snow. The cold. All of this. And if the woman reaches the top, there will be Soviet guards—how she will deal with these is unknown to me. The rear wall of the fortress is within perhaps fifty meters of the cliff face. Will there be guards beyond the fortress walls? There certainly will be guards on the walls in their towers. Can the woman scale the fortress walls? Can she kill the guards? What does the woman know of electronic surveillance and monitoring equipment the Soviets use? What does she know of all of this? Very little, I think. She is dead when she reaches the top, if she is not dead before. And we still will not have gained the height of the mountain. This is what I think."

Frost lit a cigarette, cupping the flame in his hands against the wind and against observation. What bothered him most was that Subhan was likely right—and Merana would be dead. "Shit," the one-eyed man scowled against the wind-driven snow. . . .

When Merana had been gone exactly ninety minutes, the telephone in the guard house buzzed. Frost could hear it from outside and started to run toward the light, grateful for the excuse to get into the warmth. If Merana were still alive, she would be cold—very cold.

He opened the door into the guard house, seeing Akbar holding the telephone receiver, hearing the strange language, watching Akbar's face. Frost closed the door behind him, leaning against it to prevent one of the Afghanis from entering and speaking to Akbar.

Akbar hung up the phone, then looked at Frost, lighting the cigarette in the corner of his mouth. He picked away the flecks of white paper.

"We have a choice, Captain—a choice, my friend."

"The choice?" Frost lit a cigarette in the blue-yellow flame of his battered Zippo.

"I do not know certainly that they believed I was one of them. We can wait here at the bottom of this cliff forsaken by Allah for the woman, or we can try to escape. If they come here for us in force, we will die surely. But if we leave—"

Frost cut him off. "If we leave and Merana did make it to the top and did somehow get the ropes down to us, we'd be deserting her."

"Perhaps we should have had her merely blaze a trail up the mountain and drop the ropes to us from varying heights so some of us could join her."

"I asked her that. She thought it would be foolish. If she couldn't reach the top, it just increased the chances of more of us getting killed. And so she wouldn't do it."

"She is in the wrong body, this woman. She should have been a man—like the old man, Hadji. She is reckless—she is insane, I think. But she is worth much."

Frost said the words he knew were in Akbar's heart, the words in his own. "We'll wait for her, then."

"Yes, Captain, we wait for her and perhaps die down here, or live long enough to die up there."

Frost laughed, a loud laugh—he thought perhaps he was going crazy. "We're making the world safe for democracy, aren't we?"

Akbar smiled, saying only, "Yes, Captain—aren't we?"

Chapter Eighteen

Frost heard it before he saw it—the sound of the ropes snaking down to them through the swirl of snow that punctuated the darkness above. He stepped back from the rock face as the ropes fell: two ropes, one on his left, one to his right, spaced perhaps three meters apart. Rocks were weighted to the bottoms to assure their drop.

"She has made it," Subhan smiled.

Frost looked at the Mujahedin leader. "Yes—did okay for a woman, didn't she?" He walked away without an answer. Behind the smile he'd flashed Subhan, there were misgivings. What if she had been captured or killed and the ropes dropped merely to entice them up the rock face? An ambush? He doubted the sound of gunfire could have been heard through the snowy night from the great distance above. He quickened his pace, toward the guard house and to alert Akbar. . . .

Because of his Russian fluency, and because so far it seemed at least that his earlier telephone conversation had been accepted, Akbar would remain behind, and with him two of the men. Subhan and Frost were to take the leadership once they reached the top and began actual penetration of the fortress. Frost stood now at the base of the rock face, a rope entwined around him which he attached to the rope to the left, one of the two climbing ropes Merana had let down—he hoped. He would be the first up, Subhan the last, the men spacing themselves ten minutes apart on the ropes, in the space of an hour then twelve men hitting the ropes and starting the climbs, the actual climbing time with the aid of the rope to be perhaps fifteen minutes. Allowing for problems, within the space of three hours, all the men would be on the plateau and in hiding.

Frost wrapped his fists around the rope and started his right foot against the rock surface, giving a glance to Subhan. The Mujahedin leader nodded. It was the reverse of rappelling, a protracted, stooped-over walk where a wrong footfall could mean death. The rope which girded his body was there simply to allow him to clip onto a piton in order to rest if necessary. Hand over hand, looking below him once, at Subhan and the others, he started up, to his right one of Akbar's men climbing the parallel rope. . . .

The one-eyed man glanced below him—he could no longer see the ground through the swirling snow, the rope already coated with a thin film of ice. Frost looked to Akbar's man on his right. The man was perhaps twenty feet below him, moving more cautiously than the one-eyed man himself moved. It wasn't bravery. It was eagerness to reach the top and get the climb done with. Frost admitted it to himself—the climb was terrifying.

With each step, he expected to slip, his back aching with the enforced stooped-over position. His hands were weary, numbed; ice encrusted his beard and mustache; and where bare skin was exposed to the icy wind, his flesh was numb as well.

He moved on, judging himself half way up the rock face, each second ticking by as he glanced at the luminous black face of the Rolex Sea-Dweller heightening the risk of detection from the Soviets above. Still Frost could not see the top of the rock face, the swirling snow limiting visibility to about fifty feet. He moved on—right foot, left foot, right foot, left foot. He moved his hands, keeping them perpetually cupped, not daring to flex them lest he lose the power to close them tightly again. Ice chips broke off the rope under his hands. He kept going.

The one-eyed man stopped, the snow swirling for an instant in a bone-shattering gust of wind. He squinted into the wind. Perhaps twenty-five feet above, he could make out the outline of the edge of the plateau. He looked down, turning his face from the wind. Akbar's man was coming ten meters back. Frost snorted against the wind, turning out of it again as he sucked in his breath, then he started upward again, hand over hand, one foot behind the other. . . .

Frost stopped again, judging himself perhaps three feet below the lip of the plateau, hanging there, waiting as Akbar's man continued the climb. Frost released a hand from the rope for a moment, raising a finger to his lips as Akbar's man looked up, giving the man the universal symbol for silence. Akbar's man nodded. Frost kept his hand free a moment longer, smudging snow from the crystal of the Rolex. The climb had taken twelve minutes. He gripped the rope for a long moment, then freed his right hand again, swinging the KG-99 around on its sling to his chest. Then he gave the web sling a solid tug to tighten the weapon there. He gripped the rope, waiting for Akbar's man again. Was Merana up there and still alive? He mentally ticked away the seconds as Akbar's man reached a parallel height. The man looked at Frost searchingly, Frost signaling him to wait, to catch his breath. They hung there, in the howling of the wind, the swirling snow covering the creases in their clothing, their gloves, sticking to Frost's eyebrows and beard. The beard itched him and he would be happy to shave it again—if he ever got the chance, he thought soberly.

Then the one-eyed man gave Akbar's man a signal and both of them started the remaining three feet to the lip of the plateau. Frost peered up, over the top. He saw nothing but the white lights from the guard houses on the fortress walls and the massive chainlink walls themselves, behind them corrugated metal—he guessed it was of a heavy enough gauge to stop most rifle slugs. He saw no sign of Merana.

"Shit," the one-eyed man rasped. Then he pushed himself up onto the plateau, going flat as searchlights from the guard towers swept across the snowy ground. Frost shuffled snow onto his back and legs, lying as still as possible, the light sweeping over him, not stopping.

Akbar's man was coming up and Frost signaled the man to the ground. The man nodded. Frost started forward, crawling on knees and elbows, the KG-99 held up and out of the snow, the chamber loaded, only the safety still on as a precaution. As he moved, he worked the knob on the bolt—the safety was off.

Frost could no longer keep from doing it—in a hoarse stage whisper, he rasped, "Merana! Merana?"

He twisted in the snow, bringing the KG-99 to bear. Crouched in the snow beside him was the girl, her eyebrows and the part of her hair that showed at the front of her shawl crusted with snow, her cheeks gleamingly red, her hands clutched on the AK-47, the knuckles red, bruised, bloody. She smiled. "Hank, you must be silent."

Frost nodded, leaning up and kissing her forehead. The flesh was cold. He signaled to Akbar's man. The man only nodded. Merana started off across the edge of the plateau, Frost following her, Akbar's man taking the end. Merana dove, up and over a snowbank, Frost following her more cautiously; then in the next second Akbar's man rolled over, falling beside them.

"What about the towers?" Frost asked her.

"I thought you would never come. I worried."

"I worried over you," Frost told her.

"The towers will require several of us. We must wait here until all are up on the plateau. They cannot see us from the towers."

Frost nodded. "We're gonna need somebody to alert the men as they come up those ropes and onto the plateau."

Akbar's man spoke, his English broken but understandable. "Muji go—wait for Subhan and other Mujahedin."

Frost reached out, clapping the man's shoulder. "Be careful—and no gun unless your life depends on it."

"Yes, Captain," Akbar's man nodded, then peered up over the snowbank. The searchlight was finishing a sweep. He looked at Frost once, then rolled over the snowbank and was gone.

Frost and the girl sat in the darkness, punctuated by the glowing of the searchlights as they passed. The snow remained blindingly thick, glistening in huge flakes when the searchlights would catch it, the cold unbearable. Frost wrapped his arm around her shoulders, the girl sitting close to him. They waited.

Two hours passed, Frost glancing to his watch now. Five A.M., give or take, he noted. It was time to move. He signaled Subhan, having let the Mujahedin leader rest for ten minutes after the climb. Then Frost, Merana, Subhan, and three of the others started away from the snowbank, running close to the wall of chain-link and corrugated metal, flattening themselves near it but not against it, moving along its length carefully. The blowing of the snow had been their enemy on the climb but their ally ever since reaching the plateau—covering their footprints almost as soon as they were made.

He had allowed twenty minutes to move along the walls to the farthest of the guard towers, another ten for unexpected delays. At five-thirty he and Subhan and Merana would be in position with the others. The remainder of the force would be on the opposite walls—waiting.

He left three of the men by the first guard tower—among them Akbar's man Muji as the squad leader. Frost, Subhan and Merana continued on. He glanced at the Rolex, smudging snow away from the crystal—it was five-twenty-nine.

In a minute, the first sounds should be heard. He watched the second hand sweep in the dim light the search beams reflected from the snow cover. Five-thirty. There was no sound. The second hand kept moving.

Merana whispered, "The attack—it has—"

Her words were drowned in the first blast. A Soviet ATGW, the Sagger, exploded down from the mountainside overlooking the plateau, into the heart of the Soviet camp. Frost saw the impact, a billowing cloud of flame soaring skyward; then he tapped Merana and Subhan on the shoulders. Subhan had the grappling hook-tipped rope already swinging, another of the Saggers impacting. As the roar of the rocket blast died, Frost heard the whooshing sound of the rope, the hook sailing skyward over the fence and connecting to a horizontal support for the guard tower.

The fences were not electrified—at least, according to Subhan, they weren't supposed to be. This was Frost's fondest hope as he grabbed the rope and placed the sole of his right boot against the fence, starting to climb.

There was the rattle of automatic weapons fire everywhere, but loudly overhead as he reached the halfway point on the fence wall. But from below him there was answering fire, Merana using her AK-47. Frost tucked back as the body from the guard tower toppled past him, the fleeting sound of a scream echoing over the gunfire, loud as the body sailed past him.

He was to the top of the fence line now, his boots against the barbed wire stretched there, his hands tugging him up along the rope. His feet cleared, his body swinging toward the tower, his feet taking the impact, his knees buckling with it as he crashed against the framework of the tower, then swung back pendulum fashion near the wall.

He started climbing again. The going was easier using the guard tower supports to aid him, automatic weapons fire rattling at him from the ground. Frost still climbed, more of the Sagger ATGWs bursting within the compound, men running in various states of undress, all armed, tanks starting to roll within the compound itself.

"Tanks—hell, I needed that," the one-eyed man rasped to himself. He reached up to the floor of the guard tower, then starting to climb again, swinging over the fence rails there and into the guard tower itself.

He loosed the sling slightly on the KG-99 as he stepped cautiously around the guard tower perimeter, the glass there already shattered from Merana's AK fire, but the rest of it shattering as Frost tucked down. Heavy assault rifle fire was coming at him from the ground. He swung the CAR-16 forward, loosing a series of rapid three-round bursts at the ground, then stopped. He saw what he wanted, the guard tower machine gun. It was belt fed and he didn't know from exactly what war it dated, but he didn't care either—it had a trigger to pull.

Automatic weapons fire pouring up toward him, he grabbed at the link belts, pulling them from their covered metal cannisters, draping them across his body. He reached down to the mounts, twisting the machine gun free, boosting it into his hands. He braced it against his body, dropping in the end of the belt, working the bolt. He swung the incredibly heavy weapon toward the compound floor, pulling the trigger. The machine gun rocked in his hands, hammering against his rib cage. He kept firing into the troops concentrated below, into the troops running across the compound floor, feeling someone beside him. He looked and it was Merana.

"Subhan and I—we will go to the armory. Follow us when you can," she shouted. Then she sprung over the railing of the guard tower and started down, Frost glancing after her a moment. Then he swung the muzzle of the machine gun again, firing it down into the Soviet forces, trying to cut a path among them as Merana and Subhan were running for the armory.

Frost could hear heavy weapons fire from the other guard towers. He ceased his own firing and looked—the other three corner towers had his own men in them.

Frost hurtled the machine gun over the side of the wall and the belts with it, then flipped the guard tower railing, starting down the tower framework, to join Merana and Subhan at the armory. The Soviet tanks had to be dealt with.

He hit the ground, swinging the CAR-16 forward, starting to run, fire and smoke and dead Soviet soldiers everywhere.

Chapter Nineteen

Frost reached the armory doors. Others of his men were on the ground, fighting, the Soviet tanks rolling out through the main gates toward the mountain. Soviet troops began to organize in the compound into strike forces.

Frost threw himself through the armory doors as a burst of machine-gun fire hammered into the wall beside him, the bullets echoing off the armory walls as he saw the beam of the flashlight.

"Hank—more of the ATGWs. We can use them against the tanks."

Frost nodded, flattened against the wall, changing sticks in the CAR-16.

"You know how to use 'em, Merana?"

"Yes—yes, of course."

"Go to it—you and Subhan. I'm heading for the main buildings. If they do have Matt or that weapon I should find one or the other or both there. See you outside, kid." Frost stepped through the armory doorway, rolling to the ground, firing the CAR-16 toward a half dozen of the Soviet troops, a roaring sound behind him. He dove, an explosive charge spitting from the armory doorway. They'd found a Soviet bazooka as well, Frost guessed.

He pushed himself to his feet, jumping the smoking bodies of the Soviet soldiers, running across the compound.

He heard a whistling sound, throwing himself to the ground, rolling under a truck, one of the ATGWs from outside the compound impacting, a massive crater in the ground, pieces of bodies and debris raining down. The truck above him started to move.

The one-eyed man reached up, found the exhaust piping and held on. The truck picked up speed now, dragging him across the snow—but nearer to the main buildings. He kept holding on, the truck starting to turn. He inched his way back along the exhaust piping, hand over hand, reaching the muffler near the truck's rear, his hands already warming under the heavy gloves from the heat of the pipe.

Frost reached into the side pocket of his peacoat, grabbing for the old dirty boot sock he'd used to shield the muzzle of the KG-99. He balled it up, ramming it into the exhaust pipe, holding his gloved hand over it, the engine noises from the front of the truck changing rapidly, coughing and seizing. The truck skidded, stopping. Frost rolled out between the wheels, climbing to his feet. The CAR-16 was in his right fist as he ran, the sounds of the engine being revved high, then—

Frost threw himself to the ground, rolling. The engine exploded, in the next second the truck's gas tank catching fire. A fireball of orange and black billowed skyward, the driver, clothes on fire, hurtled into the snow.

Frost got to his knees, pumping the trigger of the CAR-16 in a three-round burst, putting the driver out of his misery.

He was up then, running again, the main buildings looming less than twenty yards from him now.

Chapter Twenty

Outside, the one-eyed man could hear the roaring of the ATGWs. It would be Merana and Subhan and the others working on the compound ground and the tanks outside. He could see it in his mind's eye: The tanks would be turning now, realizing there was no attack from the outside beyond the rocket fire from the mountain peak above, rolling back to attack their own compound. There would be little time.

He started forward, leaving the dead guard at his feet whom he'd killed upon entering. The main buildings were interconnected by tunnels built of corrugated metal. Frost started into the nearest of these from the central entrance, hoping to find either a hospital wing, a detention wing or a laboratory wing. In either of the first two he might find Matt Jenks—in the third he might find the Soviet weapon.

He held the CAR-16 in his right fist, low, at the hip, moving ahead in a long-strided commando walk; the first finger of his right hand was against the trigger, the selector at full auto.

A Soviet guard, then another—Frost, pumping the CAR-16's trigger, threw himself against the nearest wall, shooting again and again. Slugs hammered into the wall beside his head, sparking as metal hit metal, richocheting. But the gunfire ceased then, the guards downed.

He pushed away from the wall, breathing again, changing sticks for the CAR. He moved on, reaching the far side of the tunnel. Offices—but he froze. He had learned to recognize one set of symbols in Cyrillic alphabet during his escape from Russia and the Soviet Secret Police—the symbols for KGB.* He saw them on the first door.

The one-eyed man stepped back, leveling a savage kick at the lock, the door unmoving. He stepped back again, pumping the CAR-16's trigger, the lock disintegrating. Then he wheeled, planting a double kick into the door. The door swung open, the one-eyed man stepping aside, gunfire coming from the opposite side of the doorway.

He inhaled, focusing his energy on his right hand, then rammed the hand around the doorframe, the CAR-16 in his fist. He fired the CAR fast, the .223's impacting hard on his bent wrist, almost breaking it. He pulled the gun back. There was no answering fire— either a lucky hit on his part or a clever adversary. Frost pulled the burnoose from his head, hurtling it into the doorframe, gunfire echoing in the corridor through the door. The one-eyed man hit the floor, rolling into the doorway, firing the CAR-16, a man going down, another man stepping back, a pistol in his right fist.

Frost rolled again, pumping the CAR-16's trigger, the picture of Lenin on the wall behind the desk taking the impact, the evil face punctured, falling. The man

*See, THEY CALL ME THE MERCENARY #14, The Siberian Alternative

with the pistol fired once. Frost was on his knees now, firing another three-round burst, the KGB officer with the pistol going down.

Frost pushed himself to his feet, changing sticks in the CAR, then starting forward.

Beyond the desk was a barred gate, locked. And beyond it were detention cells.

Frost leveled the CAR, firing into the lock mechanism, then kicked at the door. It bounced, jarred, and he reached out to it, pulling the door open toward him, tiny pieces of the locking mechanism falling to the floor and making a clattering sound.

Frost stepped through.

There were faces—many faces. All of them showing their history of confinement. Hollow cheeks, hollow eyes, missing teeth, cut off lips and ears. One man's left eye was missing, burned away it seemed. Frost could recognize the work. He signaled the man with one eye to step away from the cell door, then leveled the CAR-16, firing, the door rattling. The Afghani with one eye hurtled his body against the door, the door swinging open.

The man stepped out of the cell, looked at Frost, then looked down at his hands, raising them. He looked at Frost again.

The word neither of them said, the American one-eyed man and the Afghani one-eyed man knew, was "Free!"

Frost stepped back into the office for a moment, then returned, handing the Afghani the AK-47 from one of the two dead KGB men. Frost gestured toward the cell doors and the man smiled, his front teeth broken and half of them missing as well.

135

Frost walked the length of the cell block, hearing unintelligible cries which he knew meant freedom as he heard the succession of gunshots against the locks.

He stopped at the far-end cell. A body lay on the bunk. Frost stepped to the door. The body rolled, sitting up. Frost wouldn't have recognized the face—but he recognized what remained of the hair. The nose was a pulp, the lips swollen. Black and blue marks were all over the arms and the chest. The man was naked and shivering except for a pair of stained underpants. Only the hair was the same—red, but gray-tinged, burned away on the left side of the head.

"Matt?" Frost took a step back.

"Hank—Hank Frost?"

The voice was hard to understand, but there was still a fire in the eyes, a fire Frost had known in Vietnam.

"Step back—watch out," and Frost leveled the CAR-16 at the lock, firing, the lockplate shattering. Matt Jenks stepped toward it, pushing on the door gingerly as if he expected it not to open.

"Free?"

Frost pulled the mostly shot-out stick from the CAR-16 and loaded a fresh one, handing the rifle to Jenks. "Free, Matt." Frost handed him two spare magazines. "A couple of dead Russians in the office. Take the clothes you can use and the one guy's pistol. These your men?"

"Some of them—but all Mujahedin. What the hell is—"

"We're springin' ya. Where the hell's that laser gun?"

"In the field I think—saw the APC they use it from leaving this morning—yesterday morning—I don't know. But it's not here."

"At least you were. We'll get it. You walkin' wounded or need a carry?"

There was light in the eyes still, and the cracked, swollen lips curved upward in a smile. "Walkin' wounded, pal."

Matt Jenks shoved past him, Frost feeling a smile on his own face. What they had done, Jenks would carry always—if they got out. Not just the damage to the face and body—that could be repaired with surgery, hair transplants, dental work. The inside part was worse.

Frost slung the KG-99 forward, loosing the sling for greater movement, then started back up the cell block corridor toward the office.

There were still Communists to kill—plenty of them.

Chapter Twenty-One

The blasts of the Sagger ATGWs were coming in rapid succession, the windows of the main building complex vibrating with the shock waves as Frost, Jenks—not moving well and strange looking in the mixture of Soviet uniform parts—and the freed Afghani Mujahedins reached the main entrance.

Frost unslung the KG-99, entwining the webbing around his right wrist, the black, thirty-six round flash suppressor-fitted semi-automatic assault pistol looking like something in a science fiction melodrama, Frost thought, studying it for a moment. The one-eyed man turned to Jenks. "You speak the language—translate for me."

"All right," Jenks nodded, leaning heavily against the door frame.

"Tell them we get out into the main yard of the compound and toward the rear wall. There were two ropes we used on the way up. As soon as the shooting started, one of the men I sent to the second rear wall guard tower—"

"Wait—let me catch up to you," and Jenks turned to the Afghanis, speaking rapidly, the Afghanis nodding in understanding.

"Okay, but one of them was to drop six more ropes. There's a backpack full of harnesses—Subhan brought them up with him—"

"Subhan is here?"

"Anything wrong?"

"He's a good man. Babrak ul-Raq considers him his top field commander."

"Good. When you and the men get there to the edge of the plateau, suit up in those harnesses—"

"Wait—I'll translate."

Frost waited as again Jenks' words were greeted with nods and murmurs. Then Frost went on, the rockets still roaring outside. "All right—once we hit the edge of the plateau, they suit up and clamp the harnesses to the ropes, then rappel down as fast as they can. If they never rappeled before, tell 'em good luck."

Jenks looked at Frost for a moment then nodded solemnly. He translated, the men nodding, but in some of their eyes something Frost had rarely seen in Afghanis—fear.

"Let's go. As soon as we hit the yard, Merana and Subhan should be punching a hole in that rear wall."

Jenks nodded, saying something quickly to the Afghanis, the men armed with letter openers, chair leg clubs, belts—anything that could be used to fight and kill.

Frost kicked open the double doors, then ran through, into the main yard of the compound. Gunfire was everywhere, pockets of the Mujahedin fighting with the larger Soviet forces but pinning them down. Frost broke into a dead run—glancing back once, two of the Afghani's staying back with Jenks. Frost fired the KG-99 as he ran, snapping off shots, holding the ventilated barrel shroud behind the muzzle to steady his aim. He wheeled, a trio of Soviet soldiers racing across the open area of the yard toward him. Frost snapped off the first shot, then steadying the weapon with his left hand, fired two-round semi-automatic bursts, nailing the nearer of the three men in the chest. The body rocked back onto the bayonet of the man behind him. The third man fired, Frost rolling to the ground, pumping the KG-99's trigger again and again. He dropped the man with repeated torso hits. The second man was free of the dead body of his comrade, bringing up the AK's muzzle. Frost fired; two shots crashed into the neck, the throat area suddenly crimson with blood as the body spun out, falling.

The one-eyed man was up, running, Jenks and the others even with him now. A blast louder than the others echoed across the ground. The rear wall—a section of it large enough to drive a tank through—was gone. Frost saw Merana and Subhan, running, one of the Saggers carried between them. Frost glanced toward the front gates, a tank rumbling through.

Merana and Subhan were dropping down beside the gate, setting the ATGW to fire.

"Hit the tank!" Frost shouted over the gunfire.

He shouted again. "The tank—Merana—the tank!"

The ATGW fired, Frost following its trail as it snaked across the compound grounds and toward the Soviet tank rolling through the gates. The tank stopped, the right tread breaking off, a massive dent near the right side. But more importantly than the tank being stopped was the fact the tanks behind it now were at least slowed in getting into the compound.

Frost started pumping the KG-99 again, running toward Merana and Subhan beside the hole in the rear wall. Jenks and the others were ahead of him.

The KG-99 was coming up empty and Frost rammed in a fresh stick as he ran, jamming the nearly spent magazine into his belt under his wide-open coat. Soviet soldiers were breaking from cover, running for the opening in the rear wall. Frost aimed his fire toward them, running still as they fired back, the one-eyed man reaching under his coat. He switched the KG-99 to his left hand, snatching at the adjustable sighted High Power, working back the hammer with his right thumb, then pumping the Browning's trigger as well. He shouted across the yard: "Merana, get 'em outta here!"

The girl was up and moving toward Matt Jenks, her AK spitting fire at the Soviet troops. Subhan garnered a half dozen men, laying them out beside the wall as fire support to cover the withdrawal. Frost reached the wall, diving through the massive jagged hole in corrugated metal and chainlink, onto the plateau surface. The snow was wet on his face and hands. He pushed himself to his feet, replacing the High Power's magazine with a twenty-rounder, pumping it half gone through the hole toward the Soviets. He wheeled then, racing toward the edge of the plateau. Merana was already buckling Jenks into one of the improvised harnesses, Subhan getting the others going. The sun had just started to wink over the far horizon now under the layers of snow laden clouds.

Frost reached the lip of the plateau. "Merana—

you're next!"

"No—I'm the best climber. I'll go later when most of the men are down. Hurry yourself!"

"No, dammit!"

"Subhan!"

Frost started to turn, but then felt the pain, his head. "Shit!" he screamed, slamming forward into the snow.

Chapter Twenty-Two

Frost opened his eye. The ground below him was moving and there was pain in his stomach, stiffness in his back. He looked behind him, beneath him. Feet—not his.

"You stir, Captain!" The voice was Akbar's. "Here, I will set you down."

The motion stopped and Frost felt himself being slung forward, then rested on the snowy ground.

"Akbar?"

"Yes, Captain—Akbar Ali Husnain. And you are heavier than you look, my friend."

"Where the hell is Merana?"

"She never came down. We waited until the last of the residual force made it down—there was only one of them. Merana fired out all her ammunition, then was fighting the Russians hand to hand."

"I'm going back," Frost rasped, starting to his feet. But Akbar's .38-44 Heavy Duty flashed from the hip holster, the hammer thumbing back. "I'm going back!"

"Then you too would be lost." Akbar lowered the hammer. "I will not shoot you—but another bump on the head would not kill you. She is dead. She has to be. She was fighting hand to hand with a half dozen of the Soviets. They saw her go down—fighting. It is the way she would have wanted to die."

Frost pushed himself to his feet, seeing Subhan passing him. He reached out, twisting the man around, hauling back his right fist. Subhan raised a guard but Frost saw the hole in it. Frost dropped his fist.

Subhan, his voice low, his English no better, said, "Captain Frost—it was the woman's wish that you should not die. And it is the mission." Subhan walked away.

Frost stood there on the trail, looking back toward the mountain fortress, now illuminated in the dull sunlight, the snow finally having ceased. Flames leapt skyward, and as he watched there was a fireball rising—it could only have been an explosion.

The homicidal, lonely little girl—she was dead. The one-eyed man just stood there.

He tried lighting a cigarette in the blue-yellow flame of his Zippo, but his hands shook too badly with rage.

Chapter Twenty-Three

The one-eyed man rode his animal at a good trot, keeping pace with Akbar, Subhan and the others, only Jenks slightly behind, the strain of the ride telling on him. Over his own peacoat and watchcap, Frost again wore a burnoose. And around his body, partially out of defense against the cold and partially to draw less attention to himself should they encounter travelers, he had wrapped one of the blanketlike robes. They had ridden for nearly seven hours after leaving Subhan's mountain stronghold, the snow falling steadily again. Already in sight was the village where they would learn the current whereabouts of the Mujahedin leader, Babrak ul-Raq.

After the long trek on horseback returning to Subhan's camp, Frost and the weary Jenks had spoken extensively. The Soviet weapon was an operational laser cannon. It could fire with the rapidity of a machine gun and used some type of self-charging solar batteries as its power source, with a converter which stepped up the voltage. Calling it a cannon was really incorrect, Jenks had said finally. The beams of laser light it fired were almost hairline thin, but of sufficient power that repeated hits into the same area—pulses, Jenks had called them—could destroy armor plate on the most sophisticated tank. It could be mounted any-where, Jenks had said—used from aircraft, from tanks and perhaps as a ground weapon like a heavy machine gun.

During his questioning, Jenks had noted what he could, piecing together the information in the faint hope he would find a way of getting it out to U.S. Intel-ligence. He had given up on his own life weeks earlier. The weapon was a prototype—one of only three that existed and the only actually operational model. If it could somehow be stolen, it would be easy enough for American scientists to duplicate, but its mere destruc-tion would be useless. The trick was in the power con-version system, not the laser technology itself. It was this power conversion system which gave the weapon its awesome utility.

To steal it would require an assault on a Soviet armored column, or perhaps a full scale assault on a Soviet base. For this, the comparatively meager forces of Subhan would not be enough. It would require Babrak ul-Raq to commit his own forces. Jenks esti-mated some five thousand men would be needed. And the Soviet weapon's testing period was nearly com-plete. In a week or less it would be flown back to the Soviet Union, the last phase of its testing something Jenks had never been able to ascertain. For this, Babrak ul-Raq might also be of help. His intelligence network was a good one, and a lasting one because none of the network ever engaged in even the most covert acts of sabotage against the Soviets—they used KGB tactics against the KGB, as the perfect moles.

Akbar rode at the head of the column, his man Muji

146

beside him. Frost avoided the company of most of the Afghanis since the loss of Merana. It was a thing where the one-eyed man felt he had to blame someone. He blamed the Afghani warriors themselves—the duplicity of penalizing her as a woman, then letting her die more bravely than any man.

He cupped the flame of his Zippo in his gloved hands, lighting a cigarette. He was tired of the whole thing, the almost countless days of travel, the cold, the entire war. But to leave the Soviet weapon behind would have been signing his own eventual execution, he knew. With such a weapon, Jenks' statement from his last report would be an understatement—bringing the West to its knees.

The one-eyed man rode on.

Babrak ul-Raq—his English excellent—said, "It seems abundantly clear that if I and my men can be of service in this, the logical time is as Captain Frost suggests. We must take the weapon as it is about to be flown out. We eliminate then, the problems of trying to disassemble the weapon and smuggle it out a piece at a time. Matt Jenks is an accomplished flyer and—"

"Wait a sec, Babrak," Jenks interrupted. "I can fly most anything the U.S. had up until ten or twelve years ago. But whatever the hell kind of plane the Reds will be using—hey, I don't know."

"If it is the will of Allah that this weapon be taken from the hands of the Soviet invaders, then I am certain that you will find the skills with which to operate the airplane correctly, Mr. Jenks. And if it is not the will of

Allah, then all of our efforts are futile at best."

Frost couldn't pass it up. Looking at Jenks, he said, "He told you good, Matt!"

Babrak ul-Raq laughed. Jenks didn't.

"I have flown single-engine planes. Perhaps I can be of service to Matt Jenks in his efforts as well," Akbar offered.

"I landed a plane once with some coaching—but I don't know a damn thing about them," Frost volunteered. "Scariest thing I ever did in my life. Nuclear weapon aboard—but it's a long story."*

"Then it is agreed," Babrak ul-Raq said, spreading his hands, smiling. "If we do this thing, it will be done at the airfield from which the Soviet weapon will leave for Moscow."

"Can your intelligence network find out when—where?" Frost asked.

"This can be done, I believe, with no little degree of difficulty, certainly, but done expeditiously nonetheless. The crux of the entire matter, as I interpret the situation, seems rather than the means being in question, it is the motivation."

Frost sighed hard. "Such a weapon could wreak terrible devastation on your people. I understand that to a degree it already has. It could bring devastation upon my people as well, giving the Soviet Union a sufficient edge that they might actually take steps toward all-out war. Then we might all die, or certainly suffer."

"There is little to refute in your rationale, Captain Frost," Babrak ul-Raq nodded. "Yet, I must risk the lives of many of my field agents and once the informa-

See, THEY CALL ME THE MERCENARY #5, Canadian Killing Ground

tion required is satisfactorily obtained, I further place in jeopardy the lives of several thousand of my men. And—" he raised the first finger of his right hand beside his face for emphasis—"such an attack on such an unprecedentedly massive scale would indeed require the relocation of my headquarters, perhaps the dispersal of my forces into the deeper recesses of the mountains to avoid Soviet punitive expeditions."

"May I be blunt, Babrak ul-Raq?" Frost asked.

"Indeed you may. We speak as allies here rather than adversaries, Captain."

"Are you asking for economic or military assistance to alleviate the hardships you foresee?"

"There are means," Babrak ul-Raq smiled, "of smuggling weapons into this area. Many are acquired even now through a variety of means—if my meaning is clear?"

Frost only nodded.

"I have here a list—one you might choose to memorize—you and Matt Jenks. Any of these items which might be provided—as a gesture of good will by your government to aid our efforts—would be received with heartfelt thanks."

"That's it?"

"Yes—but here is my list, Captain."

Frost took the neatly folded piece of heavy paper as Babrak ul-Raq withdrew it from under his coat. The one-eyed man opened it, looking at it. In beautifully written English, it resembled, Frost thought, a Christmas list.

"Dear Santa," Frost began, ul-Raq himself laughing. The one-eyed man recognized the nomenclature for nearly all the items listed—electronic surveillance equipment, night vision equipment and the like. It was the sophisticated weaponry of warfare ul-Raq required, not guns and ammunition. Frost looked up from his perusal of the list, saying, "I shall memorize it. Then, if I'm successful in leaving Afghanistan, I'll recite the list to the most influential persons I know. Matt," and Frost handed the list to Jenks. "I'm sure Matt will do the same. Beyond that—" Frost shrugged.

"We are men of good will," Babrak ul-Raq smiled. "And such an assurance is bond enough. I shall undertake immediately to have the information acquired necessary to the completion of this operation."

Frost nodded. He realized the interview was over, really, as ul-Raq clapped his hands and a woman appeared in the next instant carrying a tray of tiny cups. Tea time? Frost wondered.

After refreshments, Frost, Jenks and Akbar left the tent. Akbar stopped Frost as they were halfway across the compound grounds, saying, "For an American, your English is very good—nearly as well-spoken as that of Babrak ul-Raq, Captain."

Frost stopped walking, looking at Akbar for a moment. "Thanks a hell of a lot, pal."

The one-eyed man just kept on walking.

Chapter Twenty-Four

"You speak and understand some Russian then?"

"Very little," Frost told Akbar. "Languages were never my strong point. Now if the Spanish had invaded Afghanistan and I were going to pose as a Spanish officer, I might have a chance. I can 'habla' along a little with it." Frost looked at Akbar.

"I speak Spanish, Captain. I understand your meaning—but the pun was not funny. I am very sorry, Captain."

Frost sneered, then said, "So you're going to teach me the right things to say?"

Akbar grinned now. "Yes—with the way I look, even with my beard shaved away as it will be, I could not pass for a Soviet officer, but for a Soviet enlisted man perhaps. When we penetrate the air base, Matt Jenks as our prisoner, you will be the leader. I will endeavor to do as much of the talking as possible in Russian, but you will have to know a few key phrases, Captain. This will be vital."

"Sometime—if we get out of this—I'll tell you what happened to the last person who tried teaching me Russian—a woman."* Frost lit a cigarette. "Okay, I'm game."

*See, THEY CALL ME THE MERCENARY #14, The Siberian Alternative

151

"Very good, Captain. Now—there will be several basic situations we should encounter. Just being around such a marvelous English speaker as Babrak ul-Raq makes me so aware of my own language deficiencies. But now—at the gates to the base, it will be necessary to expect the guards to ask for identification papers. Babrak ul-Raq's team of forgers will craft these for our use. And there will be questions about our purposes at the base."

"I don't think I'm gonna like this," Frost interrupted, stubbing out his cigarette.

Two days had passed and Frost sat again in the tent of Babrak ul-Raq. "My intelligence sources have at last indicated the purpose of the final airborne tests for this laser weapon which you seek, gentlemen."

"What is it?" Jenks asked.

"Yes," Frost murmured.

Akbar remained silent as he usually did in the presence of ul-Raq.

Babrak ul-Raq sighed long and heavily. "It appears I would have been militarily engaged on a grand scale regardless of helping your pursuits. The Soviets are planning a major offensive to begin within three days. The laser weapon will be mounted aboard one of their old-style fighter bombers which has been modified to accept a bubble dome-type gun turret. Their most sophisticated Foxbat fighter aircraft will accompany it to guard it. When the Soviet ground offensive begins the laser equipped plane will fly as its vanguard. The Soviets realize full well that a major offensive directed at population centers which they do not control would be met with heavy resistance—large concentrations of the Mujahedin in their path. The laser weapon would be used from the air on Mujahedin positions, destroying resistance to Soviet ground forces before it could be of any significant effect. The Soviet forces would take the positions they seek unchallenged. So it appears I do Afghanistan a greater favor than realized by helping in your efforts to extricate the laser weapon from Soviet hands. You may forget my Christmas list as you called it, Captain Frost."

Frost felt himself smile. "I don't think so. Sounded like pretty useful stuff you wanted. I'll remember it."

"You may feel differently," ul-Raq smiled. "In such circumstances, what is of paramount importance is the moment—not the future. If the weapon can be stolen, excellent. But if there is any doubt, those of my men who will accompany you will be under the strictest orders to destroy the weapon so it cannot be used during our resistance to the offensive—and to destroy you should you wish to prevent them from doing this."

Frost said nothing for a moment, then, "A counter proposal, then. What if we steal the weapon and the aircraft and turn the weapon on the Soviet ground forces? Kiss off their offensive, right? If the laser cannon will work on you, it'll work on them too."

"This thought had crossed my mind as well, Captain!" ul-Raq exclaimed with a smile. "Such a move would be exceedingly dangerous, however. The Foxbat fighter escort will not cross much beyond the Pakistani border. If you tarry instead in the skies of

Afghanistan, most assuredly you will encounter heavy resistance in the air. You will likely die, Captain."

The one-eyed man lit a cigarette. "I'll take my chances." Brave sounding words, Frost thought—but he was scared to death. He had never liked flying anyway.

Chapter Twenty-Five

At least the rank was correct, Frost thought, inspecting himself in the Soviet Captain's uniform. He slipped the Cobra shoulder rig over the uniform tunic, the Metalifed High Power his friend Ron Mahovsky had customized for him already holstered in it. He took the KG-99, slinging it cross body, under his right arm, then took the roll of adhesive tape, taping the gun, magazine out, against his right side to the uniform tunic. He reached down and picked up the officer's great coat and slipped it on, leaving it open. There was no such thing as a full-length mirror in ul-Raq's camp, but Frost had the hand mirror he used for shaving and moved it as best he could to ascertain that the great coat covered the two guns and all the spare magazines secreted about his body. It looked as though it would serve.

He snatched up the Soviet officer's chopka with the red star, wanting to spit on it rather than wear it. But he put it on, leaving the eyepatch in his uniform pocket and setting in place instead a pair of sun glasses he had traded one of ul-Raq's officers to get. The trade had been for the Gerber knife, but Frost felt under the circumstances the dark-lensed glasses would serve him better.

He walked from the tent. Akbar, already uniformed, snapped to attention, rendering a salute, in Russian saying, "Comrade Captain!"

Frost looked at Akbar, then both men began to laugh.

"What do you think, Akbar?"

"Very Soviet-looking, Captain—very. As long as your mouth remains as closed as possible, we have a slight chance. Your language ability is not that bad, but you forget so easily."

Frost lit a cigarette, using matches rather than his Zippo lighter, the cigarette Russian, long filtered to be smoked with gloves. He hated the taste. "Well, I'd been thinking about doing something about my memory once."

"But you forgot what it was," Akbar laughed.

"No, no—nothing like that. In fact, I saw this ad in a magazine—promising instant memory improvement. But—well, I forgot what magazine I saw it in and couldn't remember the name of the company."

Akbar smiled. "Laughing in the face of death, are we not?"

"Yes," Frost nodded. He looked beyond Akbar, across the compound which was virtually denuded now, so many of the men gone to swell the forces of ul-Raq's resistance to the Soviet offensive. But coming from the opposite side was Matt Jenks and with him Subhan and fifteen of Subhan's men. Subhan and the men were all dressed in Soviet uniforms of varying rank, only Jenks dressed in civilian clothes.

After a moment, Jenks stopped in front of Frost, saying, "You look good enough to pass, Hank."

Frost smiled. "I hope so, Matt."

"If you get outta this and I don't—well, tell Margaret and my son, tell 'em—"

Frost nodded. "There's a woman in Atlanta named Bess Stallman—you tell her the same thing, huh?"

Jenks nodded, then extended his hands, saying, "May as well get it over with, Hank."

Frost looked to Akbar and nodded, Akbar taking the Soviet handcuffs and stepping toward Matt Jenks, then clamping them on his wrists.

"Seems like I've done this before," Jenks smiled.

"The last time—one way or the other," Frost murmured. "The last time."

Chapter Twenty-Six

They had driven through the passes along the winding mountain road in the stolen Soviet vehicles for some time, and though Frost had no idea of what transpired in the truck carrying Subhan and his fifteen men, Frost had felt the silence in the car in which he rode with Akbar and the handcuffed Matt Jenks as oppressive.

As Frost lit another of the Russian cigarettes—likely taken from the body of a dead Russian—Akbar began to speak. "The Afghanis perhaps fight so fiercely because of course they have been invaded before. In 1839 the British invaded India and also took over in Afghanistan. But by 1842 the British had been driven from Kabul and the British military forces as well as escaping British civilians were slaughtered, nearly to the last man. The British invaded again in 1878—but by 1919 were forced to grant independence. The Afghanis realize this, I think, that if they fight and continue to fight, no invader will ever survive them. The tenacity of an invader can wax and wane, but the tenacity of a man fighting to make himself free does not."

Frost looked at Akbar. "What does a man with your mind—"

"Why am I a fighter? I was born a fighter—a quick

mind and someone teaching me to read were merely accidents. I am a Pathan of the Afridi first and always. I would cease in what I do if the Khyber Pass and the reason to guard it should no longer exist, perhaps. But in secret I think that were the reason to fight gone, then I too would be gone."

Frost smiled. "I give up—where did you hide your sword?"

"Ahh—you noticed it missing, Captain. The door panel of the car in which we ride slips out so easily. It would be thoughtless to leave such a marvelous recepticle unused." Akbar began to laugh, Frost joining him, but then turning to Jenks.

"What's the matter, Matt?"

"Nothing," he said, almost breathless.

"Mr. Jenks, we are friends, comrades in arms—there can be—"

"It's the damn KGB!" Jenks blurted out finally. "They'll be there and I won't let 'em get me again!"

Frost stubbed out the Russian cigarette, the taste bad, breaking down and lighting one of his own—he could get rid of the butt. "Matt," he said, a cloud of smoke exhaling in two streaks from his nostrils. "Matt—man, I don't—"

"There is perhaps one word in the languages of the Afghan people which Captain Frost understands—and you would be well to know it," Akbar said, staring over the steering wheel and along the snow-packed road. "It is 'turel.' I think you know the word, Mr. Jenks— bravery? You showed it in resisting the KGB before— and the bravery you have must truly be boundless to endure what you have endured. If it makes you rest

159

more easily, I will swear to you if you like that I will myself kill you should your capture seem inevitable. Would this comfort you, Mr. Jenks?"

Jenks didn't answer—he just shivered.

Frost wondered if, someday, this frightened, mutilated man would be him?

Chapter Twenty-Seven

Akbar drove not simply because he was a competent driver but because of the enlisted man's uniform. He stopped the car now at the entrance to the Soviet base. "Far from here," Akbar murmured, "in the desert there blows a wind—the black wind. It is called Siah Bad. It is a deadly wind. Subhan has told me that is the name given by Babrak ul-Raq's fighting men to the planes which fly from this base—Siah Bad. A black wind—the squadrons here with their ships painted black except for the red Soviet star and their other markings, they encourage the idea."

"Like the Flying Tigers in China," Frost mused, watching the door to the guard house, waiting for the gate guards to come out and the thing to begin. "The Chinese viewed the tiger as a good luck symbol, if I remember correctly, and the Japanese thought of the Tiger Shark as a bad omen. So the Tigers painted gaping mouths of Tiger Sharks on the noses of their fighters."

"I have heard of this—yes," Akbar nodded, beginning to roll down his driver's side window. The guard house door opened, two men stepping out into the cold, their breath steaming in large clouds as they did.

"Here we go," Frost said, through his clenched teeth.

161

"Yes," Akbar nodded.

The assault was to start on the base as soon as Akbar and Frost had the base gates opened for them, Frost holding under his left thigh against the seat a small radio-signal beeper. The guard approached the driver's side window. Though Frost's ability to speak Russian was as bad as he claimed, with the affair in Moscow* and Akbar's instruction, the one-eyed man felt competent in understanding the language in sufficiently broad terms to follow a conversation. He could follow this one.

The guard asked for Akbar's papers. Without Akbar turning to look, Frost reached under his coat and produced the travel papers, the orders and the identification papers which branded him—Frost—Captain Yuri Nitzki of the First Infantry Battalion on special detached duty to the Committee For State Security— the KGB. Frost passed the papers to Akbar, Akbar nodding and handing them over to the guard.

The guard—tediously, slowly—began unfolding the papers to inspect them.

The guard said that any entry to the base had to be cleared by the KGB. Akbar started to speak, Frost cutting him off saying the equivalent of "stupid," then Akbar continuing, saying that the American prisoner, Matt Jenks, was needed near the aircraft with the laser weapon because of suspected sabotage. Frost glared at the guard, the guard impassive, shaking his head, taking the papers and walking away.

"What do we do, Captain?" Akbar said through his teeth.

*See, THEY CALL ME THE MERCENARY #14, The Siberian Alternative

"Wait and see—maybe the KGB approval is a rubber stamp—just that. Maybe not. We wait and see. If there's any trouble we start shooting, drive through the gates and just hold 'em a little longer until ul-Raq's men get out of the hills. Nothing else to do."

"Look," Jenks voice rasped.

Frost glanced at Jenks, then followed the man's stare. "It's him," Jenks said. "That bastard Igorovitch—he's the one who did all this to me—personally."

It was the man who had incited the crowd in Pakistan, framed Frost for the rape of the Moslem girl, the man known as Klaus Igorovitch. "Shit," Frost murmured.

If there was one man in the KGB in Afghanistan who would instantly know Frost was Frost and not Captain Yuri Nitzki, it was Igorovitch.

"Okay," Frost murmured, watching the KGB man approaching from the far side of the gate. "Akbar, count to three and stomp that gas pedal—right through the gates."

Frost slung the KG-99 forward from under his coat, finding one of the thirty-six-round magazines under his uniform tunic. He shrugged out of the greatcoat and rammed the magazine home, working the bolt.

"Three!" Akbar shouted the word, the car lurching forward, Frost pushed against the seat back. Fishing a fragmentation grenade from the pocket of the greatcoat, he pulled the pin, lobbing the grenade through the open window on Akbar's side, past the man's face.

"I am glad you have a good aim, Captain!" Akbar shouted, the roar of the engine louder now, then drowned in the explosion of the grenade beside the guard house.

"Watch your eyes," Frost shouted, throwing his left forearm across his face as the sedan crashed against the gates. He could hear it, see it as he squinted over his arm, electrical arcs dancing across the hood of the car. "Don't touch anything metal!"

The gates ripped, tore, bent and fell as the sedan hesitated, then lurched ahead, Frost twisted in the seat now, throwing off the Soviet officer's cap, ripping open the collar of the uniform, leveling the KG-99 as he rolled into the back seat. Matt Jenks had already freed himself of the handcuffs and cranked down his window. Frost fired toward the KGB man Igorovitch. Igorovitch was getting shakily to his feet, a hole in the concrete beside the guard house where the grenade had hit. Igorovitch grasped his left arm, spinning, falling, as Frost fired again. The one-eyed man had it in his left hand—the radio signal beeper. He punched the button.

The Soviet truck behind them was through the gates now as well, the tarp coverings rolling up, armed men firing in all directions under Subhan's leadership.

"Should we stay and fight with them?"

It was Akbar shouting, the car swerving wildly as automatic weapons fire poured toward it from the fence line.

"No!" Frost shouted, pumping the KG-99's trigger, the assault pistol spitting two-round semi-automatic bursts from his hands. "No—just give 'em more time to get that damned plane airborne. Cut across the field."

Jenks was pulling out the seat back as Frost edged forward, away from it. Jenks extracted an AK-47 hidden there, cranking down his window, ramming one of the AK's through and firing. Frost glanced behind them. Subhan's men were fanning out from the truck, tossing grenades, firing AK's as they ran.

"The airfield—it is up ahead. I see the plane!" Akbar shouted over the unnaturally loud roar of the car engine and the pinging sounds of gunfire hitting it.

Frost pumped the KG-99 toward the rear of the car and the vehicles pursuing it now.

"Jenks, how much vertical movement is there in that laser gun—enough to hit targets on the ground while the aircraft is warming up?"

"I think so—not close, but maybe fifty, sixty yards away. I'm not sure," Jenks shouted back.

"Akbar, get us as close to that thing as you can—hurry!"

Frost pumped the KG-99's trigger again, the gun emptied. Stuffing the spent magazine in his trouser belt, he caught up a fresh one, ramming it home, working the bolt, then firing again.

"In less than a minute, Captain, we will be there," Akbar said.

"Got ya—grenades for any personnel nearby—shoot out the tires on any Foxbats near enough!" Frost reached into the open seat back, pulling up a sack of grenades and slinging it cross-body under his left arm.

He could hear the screech of brakes as the car lurched and swerved. The one-eyed man wrenched the door handle, stepping out, taking his CAR-16 that he'd grabbed from the rear of the car and firing over the door itself toward armed guards surrounding the plane carrying the laser weapon.

Akbar was out of the car now as well, firing his AK.

"Jenks—the pack, Akbar's rifle—get it!"

Jenks shouted back, "Right—comin' out!"

Akbar fired out his AK then whipped out his killing

knife, prying with it at the door panel. The panel popped out, and Akbar ripped it out the rest of the way. His sword. Frost watched as the Pathan slung it around his body, the Pathan looking back, a grin on his face. Akbar shouted, "Now it is a fight!"

Frost laughed, in spite of himself, in spite of the gunfire and the roaring of engine noises.

In an instant, Jenks was beside him. "Got the stuff."

"Grenades," Frost shouted, reaching one out of his own bag, pulling the pin, and hurling it toward one of the concentrations of assault rifle armed Soviet soldiers. Akbar was standing, ripping a grenade from under his open tunic, throwing it, then starting to run toward the plane.

Frost pushed himself to his feet, starting to run now as well, Jenks beside him. In Frost's left hand he carried the Lowe pack with his gear stashed inside, plus extra ammo for the guns. In his right was the CAR-16, the stock collapsed, held clamped tight in his fist. His trigger finger worked it in three-round automatic bursts toward the Soviet troops.

As Akbar ran ahead, he tossed grenades, side to side, like a flower girl strewing rose petals in a wedding ceremony. The Pathan also fired his AK from his left fist.

A hundred yards to go to the plane, Frost's CAR-16 coming up empty, the one-eyed man let it drop on his sling. He snatched at grenades then from the bag hanging from his left side, pulling the pins, tossing them everywhere as he ran.

Frost wheeled, hearing a shout from behind him.

It was Jenks, the most important man, the only one who could fly them out. His left arm was bleeding

166

heavily as Frost dropped to his knees beside him, swinging the KG-99 forward, pumping the trigger at the advancing Soviet troops.

"Matt, come on," Frost shouted.

"Help me up," Jenks rasped through clenched teeth.

Frost's left hand snaked under Jenks' right armpit; in Frost's right hand the KG-99 fired steadily. Jenks swayed as he stood, Frost snatching up Akbar's Springfield from the tarmac runway surface where Jenks had dropped it when he was shot.

Frost slung the rifle over his left shoulder, then grabbed at Jenks again, running for it now.

Akbar was nearly at the plane, on one knee beside an overturned jeep keeping up a steady stream of automatic fire.

There was a massive explosion, the ground shaking under Frost's feet as he ran, the explosion coming from the main gates. Frost glanced back, an orange and black fireball belching skyward. It would be Babrak ul-Raq's men, the full-scale assault starting.

Frost pushed Jenks ahead of him, swinging the CAR-16 forward, changing sticks, dropping the empty and leaving it. Then he shouted, "Akbar, get Jenks to the plane—hurry!"

Frost didn't wait for an answer, running again, firing the CAR-16 in long, ragged bursts at the Soviet troops.

Frost felt something tear at his left side beneath the butt of the Browning in the Cobra Gunskin rig there, then a searing pain. He lurched forward, dropped to his knees, closing his eye against the pain. He shook his head to clear it, then raised the muzzle of the CAR-16, firing again, pushing himself to his feet, stumbling forward into a low run his side screaming at him.

The plane was perhaps twenty-five yards ahead of him now. Akbar had already disappeared inside with Jenks, gunfire coming from inside the airplane.

Frost dropped his CAR-16 to his side—the magazine shot out—and reached for another grenade. He pulled the pin, tossing it toward the concentration of Soviet troops running across the runway surface after him. He ran on.

There was a fusilade of gunfire—louder than the rest because of its intensity. He felt something tear at his right thigh just above the knee, then he fell forward, rolling, his hands going to his leg, a scream issuing from his lips. "Aagh!"

The one-eyed man, his jaw set, the muscles in his neck tensed, snatched at a grenade from the sack—it was almost empty. He pulled the pin, hurtling it toward his attackers. The men started to scatter but the grenade exploded, chunks of bodies flying upward, a spray of powdered tarmac and blood and scraps of flesh raining down as Frost pushed himself to his feet, grabbed his pack and ran.

The pain screamed at him not to move, the pain in his right leg and from the wound in his left side. His fingers were sticky with blood from the leg wound. He lurched ahead, shifting the KG-99 forward, firing it in two-round bursts as he limped toward the aircraft.

"Come on, Captain!"

Frost glanced toward the open cargo doors—Akbar, the AK in his hands, blazing.

Frost let the KG-99 fall to his side, running now, limping, his leg pumping blood onto the runway surface.

The plane was ten yards away. Nine. Eight.

"Come on, Captain—my friend. Come on!"

Frost threw himself forward, his arms reaching out, Akbar's rifle dropping to the sling, Akbar's hand reaching out, Frost's hand locking on Akbar's wrist. The man—more powerful than he seemed—wrenched Frost up, hauling him into the aircraft.

"Your leg," the Pathan shouted, picking up his weapon, firing at the troops on the runway surface.

Frost crawled, twisted, moved his body toward the door. He pushed the CAR-16 forward, changing sticks, then firing beside Akbar.

"All right—get something on it when you can, before I bleed to death. Help me get to the gun, Akbar."

Frost fired out the CAR-16, ripping the sling from his body, letting the rifle drop and pulling himself up to his feet using a hold on the aircraft's ribs to do it.

He heard it then—the whirring of the prop, then the roar and the whir of the second prop, the aircraft's engines coming to life.

"Good man, Jenks!" Frost shouted forward.

Akbar was ramming a fresh stick into his AK, shouting, "The laser gun is in the gunner's bubble—you must climb up into it along a narrow ladder."

"Wonderful," Frost rasped. He threw himself forward along the ribs of the aircraft, steadying himself.

"I will help you—"

"No, Akbar—better stay by the doors," Frost called out. He could see the ladder ahead, working his way along the ribs of the aircraft toward it. He fell against the ladder, looking up.

"Come on, Frost," he rasped to himself under his breath, then reached up for the ladder rungs. The pain in his side seized him.

"Shit!" He shouted, then reached again for the ladder rungs, the pain at least controllable now. He started up, slowly, dragging his right leg with difficulty.

He could see the laser gun above him, pulling himself toward it. The padded gunner's seat looked comfortable at least—he could get off his leg, let his side ease up.

He swung himself into the chair and sagged down, closing his eye against the pain, then opening it, seeing through the bubble a large force of the Soviets closing toward the plane, and the vapor trails as the Foxbats warmed their engines.

"Hell," the one-eyed man rasped.

He looked to the laser gun's controls. Jenks had told him as much as he could about its functioning and Akbar—with his good knowledge of science and skill with languages—had taught Frost the Cyrillic symbols for any possible terms necessary to the operation of the weapon. Frost searched the control panel, finding clearly marked fire control buttons inside the hand holds for the twin-barreled gun. He needed a "power-on" button—he tried to remember the symbol. The Cyrillic was so confusing to him, the letters so similar. He found a toggle switch, then hit it, the lights on the controls illuminating. There was picture-writing visible now and Frost studied it, glancing up once and seeing the advancing Soviet troops, hearing the roar of gunfire as Akbar held them off from the cargo door.

There was a targeting computer. Frost reached around and moved it out on its mounts, swinging it into position, the images he saw in the computer looking like a video game. Grids gave the images depth and direction, and apparently these images were produced by some type of light source because he could see the crude outline of the Foxbats and tiny dots in the grids—the Soviet ground troops, he surmised.

He shifted the targeting computer away again and searched the light panels and switches. There was something in Cyrillic which seemed to indicate a power booster. He hit the switch. Nothing happened.

"Akbar, come on and read this damned thing for me—hurry!" Frost shouted, giving up.

"Coming, Captain," he heard the voice call back.

There was a loud burst of gunfire, then the heavy thudding of footsteps. Frost looked down, Akbar stepping over a dead body near the base of the ladder—one of the Russians who'd been aboard the craft—and starting to climb.

"They are massing for an attack, Captain—and the Foxbats are readying as well."

"I know," Frost nodded, feeling sick with loss of blood, his right trouser leg sodden.

"Here—this button keeps the power boost on surge, to maintain power. And this is the turret release—here. So the gun will swing. Here is the fire—"

"I know," Frost told him.

"Very well—and this is elevation and range control. This ball would be moved under the left foot to control that—pneumatic, I think. All you need to do is shoot. This targeting computer should do the rest."

"All right," Frost groaned. "Get back to the cargo door and shout out for Matt to hurry it up and get us airborne."

"The engines must warm, the oil pressure—the biggest engines require sometimes the most time."

"Tell him to hurry anyway," Frost nodded.

"Your leg—before you bleed to death," and Akbar stepped down a rung and ripped the belt from his trousers, then reached under his uniform tunic again, producing his burnoose. "I am never without this, Captain. When we reach our destination, I will hold you personally responsible to purchase me the material with which to have my wife make a new one."

He looked up at Frost and grinned, the one-eyed man slapping his Pakistani friend on the back, then wincing in pain as Akbar packed the burnoose tight over the wound. "Elevate the leg at the front of the gun turret. I'll help you strap in and it shouldn't restrict your movement."

"Good idea," Frost nodded, still feeling the pressure and feeling more pain as Akbar tightened the belt over the packing to hold it in place.

"Here," and Akbar raised Frost's right leg. The one-eyed man screamed.

"You cannot do this—"

"Gotta—you can help Matt fly the plane. I can't." Frost breathed hard, saying then, "Now get me strapped in."

Akbar's hands worked the webbed harness, down across Frost's shoulders, then connecting to the waist straps, cinching the harness tight. "The wound in your side—"

"That one's okay—only hurts when I laugh!"

"Hah—you are crazy, Captain. I like you for it!"

Frost moved in the seat, his hands on the fire-control handles and his trigger fingers on the fire buttons.

"Now get outta here—they're coming."

"Allah watch over you, Captain." Akbar dropped

down the ladder and was gone.

Frost swung the gun, getting the feel of it in his hands, then reached up with his left hand to shift the targeting computer into position. His left side was still screaming at him in pain. He shifted the computer in front of his eye, then peered under it. The dots on the computer had to be the skirmishing line of the Soviet troops approaching the aircraft. Frost wondered if the thing would fly even with the bullet holes it had sustained. It would have to do.

"Allah or whoever, watch over all of us, Akbar," Frost rasped, then grasped the fire control handles tightly, his fingers over the buttons. "Eat laser light, suckers!" Frost laughed, punching the buttons. There was a beam of light barely visible in the smoke of the grenade that exploded as he fired, and the ground beside the nearest Foxbat erupted in an explosion.

"Hah hah!" Frost swung the laser cannon into position on the ground forces, then fired, then fired again and again, watching the little dots on the targeting computer disappearing. "You could make a fortune with this as a video game," he shouted, thinking perhaps the pain and the anxiety were making him crack.

He kept firing, staring under the targeting computer, seeing the Soviet soldiers bursting into flame, sometimes the bodies exploding. He guessed perhaps he was hitting loaded magazines of ammo when this happened.

He kept firing, training the gun back on the Foxbats, firing again and hitting the ground. Why wasn't it exploding? Then he realized it, as he peered intently beneath the targeting computer. The first time he had hit the maintenance gear with oil or gasoline on it or near it. He scanned under the computer as he swung the gun. He saw something that would really give an explosion—not just a small canister of oil. A fuel truck. He aimed the gun and stared under the targeting computer. "Ha!" He peered into the computer, seeing the rough outline of the fuel truck. He pressed the fire buttons, the fuel truck seeming to dissolve on the computer after a flash of brightness that almost blinded him.

He looked under the graphics display. The truck was engulfed in orange and black flame.

"Yeah," the one-eyed man rasped, feeling movement in the aircraft, the plane starting forward. He kept firing, aiming at the Foxbats on the ground, some of them already starting to taxi.

He got one in his targeting computer and pressed the fire control buttons—it was almost as if he were spectacular, like when he'd hit the fuel tanker. He looked, the Foxbat invisible in a shroud of flame.

"Yeah." Frost swung onto another Foxbat, firing, but missing as he felt a lurch in the pit of his stomach, the aircraft rising visibly now as he looked past the computer. They were airborne.

Chapter Twenty-Eight

The Foxbats were getting airborne, too.

The one-eyed man swung the gun, his hands gripped like vices on the fire-control handles, his left foot working the elevation controls, his right eye studying the computer as the images of at least six Foxbats started to appear.

There were dots on the screen behind the images of the Foxbats and he assumed the dots were still more of them.

He glanced to his right and down, the shadow of the aircraft visible below him across the blown whiteness of the snow, mountain peaks rising, the plane rising as well. Frost heard a voice—English-speaking—coming over a headset beside him, then reached down and settled the headset so the microphone was beside his mouth. It was Akbar.

"Captain, are you well?"

"Yes—okay."

"Captain, there are many of the Soviet fighter aircraft approaching. What should we do? Jenks wishes to climb for—"

"Hank—" It was Matt Jenks cutting into the transmission.

"Yeah—what?" Frost studied the images in the targeting computer seeing clearly now that the smallish dots that had been behind the original six Foxbats were also Foxbats—twelve in all now.

"Hank, I wanna climb but Akbar here doesn't want me to."

"You're flyin' the plane, Matt, but I think Akbar's right. In fact, if you can keep low through these mountains between the peaks we might have a chance. I pretty much understand the rotational abilities of this laser gun. I can shoot almost directly overhead and in 360 degrees on all sides—but not directly below us. You keep this bird flyin' low enough I can count on 'em not getting under us. Then I can maybe hold 'em off."

"Captain, there is the matter of the Soviet offensive—even without the laser gun and the Foxbat escort, the Soviet troops vastly outnumber the Mujahedin forces of Babrak ul-Raq. We must dispatch these fighters quickly if we can."

"Before we help ul-Raq, I wanna get us back to that airbase and wipe out the resistance to Subhan's people. Gotta do that."

"You're both nuts," Jenks rasped through the headset. Frost decided Jenks' mouth was too close to the microphone. "We get rid of the Foxbats, we gotta get this thing over free airspace before the Reds send more stuff after us."

"I made a promise, Matt—to Subhan, to ul-Raq—just like the one I made to your wife to get you out of here if I could. I like to keep promises."

"Like you said, Hank—I'm flyin' the plane."

Frost said nothing for a moment. Jenks was reacting to the KGB torture sessions, to the demoralization. And Frost had to settle it quickly—the Foxbats were

176

getting within missile range of him, he guessed.

"Akbar," Frost sighed into the microphone.

"Yes, Captain—yes?"

"Akbar—Matt's to fly this thing low, between the peaks. If he doesn't, and if he doesn't turn it around after I shoot the Foxbats out of the sky or lose 'em—"

"Yes, Captain?"

"Take one of those pimpy old revolvers of yours and shoot him in the right kneecap."

"Can't fly the plane all shot up, Hank."

The Foxbats were closing—fast. "Right," Frost nodded to the headset. "Right, Matt—fuzzy thinking on my part. Akbar?"

"Yes, Captain?"

"Forget about shootin' him. Take your killing knife and start cutting off pieces of his body. Start with the outside of his right ear—not much blood loss and he should still be able to fly."

"Yes, Captain."

The plane dipped suddenly, Frost feeling his breakfast rising in his throat, the mountain peaks suddenly surrounding him in the gunner's seat and no longer below him.

"And it's not because you're gettin' this whacko to carve pieces out of me!"

Frost felt a smile, rasping into his headset microphone: "Matt, I knew you could. It's your play in the cockpit. I'll be hanging on the gun here no matter what you do."

"Got ya!"

"Captain, as I said before—the blessings of Allah—"

Frost didn't answer.

The Foxbats were opening fire.

His hands tightened on the firing handles, his trigger fingers poised over the firing buttons.

"Eat laser light, suckers!" He pressed the firing buttons, the nearest of the Foxbats coming in fast and the computer grids locked over it. There was a blinding flash on the screen of the targeting computer. A Foxbat passed overhead, Frost rotating the gun, tracking it on the computer grids. "Come on, baby," he rasped, the grids locking over the target, his fingers pressing the firing buttons. The aircraft exploded.

He heard a roar, a missile coming for him, saw it in the computer and fired instinctively. The missile was a hit. The aircraft rocked, Frost swaying with the gun, then rotating it, shouting, "Yeah—all right!"

Another missile came at them and he fired again, making another hit. Then he swung the gun toward the nearest of the Foxbats, tracking it, but hearing the roar again—another missile. He swung the gun, acquiring the target, firing, the missile exploding. Frost looked up as the aircraft rocked, the glass of the gunner's dome smudged black in spots.

He swung the laser cannon again, swinging almost a full 180 degrees—another Foxbat. It was in the grids and he fired, hearing the whoosh of a missile, swinging round another ninety degrees, firing as he acquired the target, then swinging the gun onto another of the Foxbats. He fired again, the Foxbat still coming. It was his first miss. He fired again, hitting, the Foxbat exploding. Frost looked up, a large chunk of wing, burning, tumbling toward him and rolling across the top of the bomber's fuselage inches from his face and the glass which shielded it.

He swung the gun, the targeting computer showing

two of the Foxbats closing, then breaking off.

"Tricky bastards," he rasped, taking the target on his left first and firing, then hearing the whoosh of a missile. He rocked the gun hard right, firing, getting the missile. Hearing another roar, tracking onto the missile, he leveled up onto the Foxbat first, disintegrating it. Then he tracked the missile. He fired, the impact rocking him in the gunner's seat, the plane lurching violently.

The aircraft was rolling—Frost could feel it, see it, staring below for an instant at the side of a mountain, snow drifting in huge windborne clouds from the prop drafts. He looked back to the computer—another Foxbat, a missile and yet another missile. He took the nearest missile, then the next, hearing another roaring sound, then tracking onto a third missile, hitting it, then tracking to a fourth, hitting it as well.

Bullets hammered through the Plexiglass of the bomber's gunner's bubble. Frost felt the impact as machine-gun slugs tore into his seat, glass spraying onto his pants. The Foxbat was coming, firing its guns. More of the dome was shot away, Frost feeling the bone chilling cold suddenly, then locking the grids over the Foxbat fighter, firing the laser gun.

The Foxbat exploded.

He'd lost count of the number of kills, firing again as a missile was launched against him, tracking still another missile, getting it and simultaneously acquiring the Foxbat that fired it. The plane was coming in fast, the image on the computer growing to where it almost consumed the entire screen. Frost fired the laser cannon, the Foxbat exploding, the glass of the dome exploding as well. Frost shielded his face with his arms.

The wind whipped at him, the cold numbed him, his hands reaching out blindly for the firing handles, his fingers closing down over the firing buttons. A Foxbat was coming, rolling out of a dive, guns blazing. Frost fired the laser cannon and missed, slugs crashing into the fuselage beside him, the pinging maddeningly loud even over the roar of the slipstream. He had the grids locked, but the Foxbat rolled. Frost swung the gun, his fingers locked over the firing buttons as he abandoned acquiring the target. He would let the target acquire his guns—fly into them. He rotated the gun rapidly, seeing the plane rolling out of the grid, then elevated the gun quickly, firing, firing again, then again. An explosion—deafeningly close—rocked the aircraft. Then the Foxbat turned into a ball of flame.

Frost swung the laser gun—there were no more Foxbats. He didn't know whether he had shot them all, or if some had pulled out.

But he heard Matt Jenks and Akbar making a kind of strange static on the comm line. He guessed they were cheering.

Chapter Twenty-Nine

The one-eyed man sat uncomfortably in the gunner's seat, bundled in his peacoat, Akbar's coat and a blanket found in the plane. He was so covered up he could barely see, and still the icy wind tore at him, numbed him, the glass bubble completely shot away.

There were no more of the Foxbats in sight now; and there had been no more since his shooting of the last of the attackers after leaving the base. Now Jenks flew the plane low, the base coming into sight beyond the white of the snow. Its anti-aircraft guns would be opening up soon, perhaps more of the missiles. Frost's hands were wrapped in bits of cloth over his gloves, and still they were cold as he clamped his numbed fists over the firing handles, his trigger fingers closing over the firing buttons.

His targeting screen showed a missile coming toward him—almost casually, Frost pushed the firing buttons, the missile vaporizing in a burst of light on the computer. The one-eyed man swung the gun, watching for the profile of his own aircraft looming large in the computer as he swung the gun farther forward, the wind ripping at him.

"Shoot off my own wing—that'd be great," he said to himself, and into the microphone before him as well.

He fired, another missile that he'd picked up, the missile gone now.

"Helicopters coming, Hank!" It was Jenks through the headset.

Frost rotated the gun, across the fuselage and along the portside of the plane. "See 'em—they won't be comin' for long!"

Suddenly Frost wondered—did the thing ever run out of ammo?

He fired anyway, vaporizing one helicopter, then another and still another.

"More choppers on the starboard side, Hank!"

Frost swung the gun, "Acquired 'em, Matt!" His lips were numbing with the cold as he fired—one chopper down. Two more remained, a missile firing from the nearest one, then another and another. Frost rotated the gun, acquiring the missiles on the computer, the grids locking over them. Then his fingers worked the fire control buttons, one missile down. He swung the gun, another missile gone. He elevated, a second later firing, a third missile and a fourth as he fired again. He rotated the gun, taking aim not at the helicopter which had fired, but the last chopper, because it had missiles still. He fired as the helicopter fired a missile, the helicopter disintegrating. There was still the missile it had fired, and Frost swung the gun, elevating, firing, missing and firing again—this time a hit.

He swung the gun, the remaining helicopter starting to flee—he fired. The helicopter vanished in an explosion of light on the grids of the targeting screen.

"Closing on the base, Captain!"

"Okay, Akbar," Frost rasped, his teeth chattering. He lowered his elevation. Sighting on the base perimeter fence, he shot it away, then swung the gun, finding a shape on the computer that looked like a tank. He fired, the tank vaporizing.

It went on—weapons trained against them, artillery rounds exploding in mid-air near the aircraft. Frost swung the gun to each new target, firing, the targets disappearing from the screen in bursts of light, in balls of flame leaping from the ground.

Each truck, each tank, each building were his targets; the one-eyed man was so thoroughly numbed with the cold all he could move were the parts of his body which controlled the gun's direction. There were aircraft, scrambling, and Frost took most of these before they got airborne, shooting down the rest as they attempted to flee their own weapon, their own firepower—their own tool of destruction.

He rasped into his microphone, "That clears up the base—now let's track that offensive while I can still move."

"Roger on that—wilco, Hank." And the plane started to climb, rolling slightly. Frost felt nauseous, but afraid to vomit lest it would freeze halfway up his throat and choke him. He hugged his body with his arms, the cold destroying him.

He closed his eye. . . .

"Hank! Hank! Dammit, Hank!"

"Captain! What is the matter?"

Frost opened his eye, hearing Akbar asking, "Captain—is there something wrong?"

"No," Frost said, his lips thick. "No—passed out from the cold. How soon to target?"

"Below us, Captain!"

Frost moved his stiff arms, then settled his hands on

the firing grips, rotated the gun, his left leg moving awkwardly. The gun swung ninety degrees and down. He could see the Soviet convoy on the road below, heading toward the village where ul-Raq's headquarters were near.

"Kill some more women and children—use your fuckin' gas—take it and shove it," Frost rasped, settling his fingers over the fire control buttons. Then, acquiring his first target on the computer, he aimed for the lead truck. It was farthest away and he fired at it, the truck exploding in a burst of light on the computer. It was simple, really—he simply moved the gun slightly, all the trucks and tanks in convoy turning into bursts of light on the targeting computer, disappearing forever, the men inside them gone, dead.

Frost wondered for an instant how many men he had killed—with the convoy and the base he wondered if he could count that high. He kept firing, firing until the last of the convoy was destroyed.

"Large concentration of Soviet troops in that cleft of rock on the starboard side, Hank—maybe fifty or more."

Frost said into his microphone, his right eye closing, "Let ul-Raq's men have them—it's enough for me today. And somebody come and get me out of here before I freeze to death."

He closed his eye—perhaps because of the cold, or the loss of blood, or the lapse of tension. But almost instantly, he realized he was asleep. The dream started—Bess beside him and they were warm together. Warm . . .

Chapter Thirty

Warm. He opened his eye, the sun blindingly bright despite the sunglasses. He heard splashing sounds.

He sat up, yawning, watching against the shimmer of light off the water as Bess pushed herself up onto the edge of the pool.

She stood up, toweling her wet blond hair, the deep blue of the two-piece bathing suit deeper seeming against the tan her skin had acquired in the last two weeks.

"Waking up, Frost?" She smiled as she walked over to the lounge chair, Frost smiling at her.

"Yeah—a little, I guess. What the hell time is it?"

"You wear a watch all the time."

"Oh yeah—don't mind me. Fuzzy, you know," and he raised his left wrist, peering at the black face of the Rolex. It was two in the afternoon.

He looked back up at her standing beside him now. "What's so funny, kid?"

"You are," she smiled. "You ever look at yourself in a pair of swim trunks when you've got a tan?"

"Naw, rather look at you—why?" and he looked down at his chest and his abdomen and his legs below his dark blue trunks.

"You look like a demonstration dummy for a surgical course—all that scar tissue."

Frost smiled up at her, glancing to the left rib cage then, the scar there very white and then to his right leg, just above the knee, the scar there long, white, jagged and rather unpleasant looking.

"You ever think of keeping all the bullets they've pulled out of you—maybe in a mayonnaise jar?"

"Isn't that one of my old jokes?" he asked her.

"If it isn't, it should be," she answered, pulling the lounge chair beside him, then sitting back in it, finding her sunglasses and turning to face him. "How you feeling?" Her voice had softened.

"Fine—stiff a little in the leg, but fine."

"You're lucky you weren't a stiff. You were starting to get frostbite—and no jokes."

"How about we go up to our room and I give you a frostbite—you know, a Frost bite?"

"I mean it—no jokes. Couldn't that Akbar guy have taken the gun so you wouldn't have been back there freezing to death?"

"Sure—hey, Akbar, you take the gun—you freeze. I don't want to any more."

"You know what I mean."

"Hey, I should marry you. You already nag me anyway."

"Yes, you should." She leaned toward him and kissed him hard on the mouth. "I love you—despite the fact you go out all the time to get yourself killed. One of these days you'll succeed at it if you don't get careful."

He faked a Western drawl, saying, "A man's gotta do what a man's gotta do."

"I wasn't talking about excretion—I was talking about common sense, Frost."

"Well, we got nothin' to do for a while—just soak up the Florida sun and rest, recuperate—"

"You spend half your life recuperating. I'm only saying it because I love you, don't want you killed."

"I know, kid." He smiled, reaching to the table beside him, finding his battered Zippo and his pack of Camels. He lit a cigarette in the blue-yellow flame, Bess promptly taking it, nodding her thanks.

He shook his head, laughing, his left side hurting slightly when he did, then lit another cigarette for himself.

"Why don't you buy your own cigarettes?"

"Why should I? Smoking is bad for you—so I'm helping you out by taking yours. They taste better than mine, anyway."

"Yeah—I'd walk a mile for a—"

"Captain Frost?"

Frost saw the shadow blocking the sun and looked up.

"Plaskewicz!" Frost got to his feet, the wound in his side giving him a stitch of pain as he stretched his right hand, the CIA man taking it. "How are things in Islamabad?"

"You're the one?" Bess asked, her voice tinged with menace.

Frost glanced at her, putting his right arm around her waist as she stood beside him.

"Guilty," Plaskewicz smiled. "And you must be—er—"

"Yeah—she's Bess," Frost laughed.

"A pleasure to meet you then," Plaskewicz smiled.

"This isn't just coincidence—I mean it can't be. The same hotel in Miami, the same—"

"No, Miss Stallman, it isn't coincidence."

"Shit," she murmured, Frost looking at her, shaking his head. "I don't know why you're here, Mr. Plaskewicz—at least not exactly why, but he's still recovering from the last—"

"Shh—let the man talk," Frost told her. "I won't do anything stupid or anything."

"What, a character change?"

"Relax," Frost smiled, holding her more tightly. Then he turned to Plaskewicz. "But she's got a point. I'm still mending from the other thing."

"I know that. Can we talk—inside? Maybe at the bar?" Plaskewicz shook his suitcoat at the lapels. "Hot out here—I'm not used to warm weather."

"Bess—" Frost began.

But she interrupted him. "Me, too," and she reached down to the back of the lounge chair and snatched up a dark blue terry-cloth wrap, Frost holding it for her. It came to mid-thigh and she belted it tightly around her waist as she stepped into a pair of sandals. "I'm ready."

Frost looked at her and laughed. "I don't say nothin' without no lawyer, Plaskewicz." He snatched up his dark blue knit shirt and pulled it on over his head, then stepped into the deck shoes beside his chair, catching up his cigarettes, lighter and room key from the table. "You buyin'?"

"My uncle is," Plaskewicz smiled. Frost started after him then, holding Bess by the hand—thinking he was doing it to keep her from biting the CIA man. . . .

They sat in a dark booth at the end of the bar, Frost sipping at a glass of Myers's dark rum—like his pal O'Hara always drank—and Bess drinking a gin and tonic. Plaskewicz had a beer.

"So," Plaskewicz smiled. "Good to see you thawed out. After you got in with that plane, I thought you were a snowman or something," and Plaskewicz laughed—the laughter was forced.

Bess spoke. "Mr. Plaskewicz. It's nothing personal. But what do you want?"

Plaskewicz sipped at his beer before answering. "Him," and he looked at Frost. "I want him for a job. Not much of a job, but one that wants doing well—one only he can do really."

"Bullshit," Bess murmured.

"Both of you," Frost said finally, lighting a Camel in the blue-yellow flame of his Zippo, the lighter's flame dancing in the current of the air-conditioning, and inordinately bright in the darkened bar. "Look," said Frost, turning to Bess, "let's hear the man first, then see, huh?"

She nodded, not looking at him, her eyes fixed like daggers on Plaskewicz.

"So what do you want from me?"

Plaskewicz nodded. "You delivered really good on that—that device. Our people have checked it out, are duplicating it, and probably now neither side will use it—at least not for the foreseeable future anyway. I guess I figured you'd want to wrap up the loose ends. You remember Klaus Igorovitch?"

Frost nodded. "The one who carved on Matt Jenks and if Merana survived long enough probably killed her. The one who set me up for that rape of the Moslem girl. I remember the son of a bitch."

"Who's Merana?"

Frost looked at Bess and said, "The sixteen-year-old girl I told you about, the one who went down swinging at the Soviet troops—"

"Okay," and she squeezed his hand under the table.

"So what about him?" Frost asked Plaskewicz.

"I'm here to debrief you on any last-minute details you might have remembered. That's why Uncle's payin' the check. Not for this—this is personal. I shouldn't even tell you this. You and Matt Jenks were pretty good friends. So I figured you'd wanna know. They got him—probably gonna get you, too."

"Who?" Bess asked. "This Igorovitch—"

"The KGB," Frost whispered to her.

"The KGB—yeah," Plaskewicz answered, his voice low. "But not really. See, agencies can't usually afford to go in for grudge warfare with each other. But Igorovitch—he went out on his own. Now usually the parent agency would stop him, but he's getting rid of some potential embarrassments for them anyway—and the KGB isn't too fond of you after that deal in Russia, anyway.* So Igorovitch killed Matt Jenks three days ago just when Matt was going back into the hospital for some cosmetic surgery on the side of his head where Igorovitch burned his hair and scalp away."

"He what?" Frost felt his woman's hand tightening on his.

"You don't wanna know the details," Frost whispered to her. "How'd Igorovitch get him, Plaskewicz?"

"Sniped out. We found the rifle—or the Anchorage police did anyway, and they got the FBI in on it. I was here already so since I was tracking you down for that debriefing thing, my boss figured I should mention it to

*See, THEY CALL ME THE MERCENARY #14, The Siberian Alternative

you. Not the kind of thing to talk about on the phone."

"How are Matt's wife and son—how they taking it?"

"The son's in protective custody—wanted to find Igorovitch himself—"

"That's Matt's kid all over. How about Margaret?"

"I think she had expected it for so long, with the time Matt was in Afghanistan, that it didn't shock her as much as it could have—I don't know. But the important thing now is that you've got Igorovitch on your ass," and he looked at Bess, smiling sheepishly. "Sorry."

"Hey—just forget I'm here. I'm just wondering if Matt Jenks' wife and I should start comparing notes," Bess rasped.

"All right—knock it off," Frost told her.

"I'm supposed to advise you to lay low, offer official protection if you want it. Until the FBI or our people track down Igorovitch. I could probably get that buddy of yours—O'Hara—to guard you if you want. You gotta figure a one-eyed man and a pretty blond woman make a reasonably easy target to locate."

"Flattery'll get you nowhere," Bess smiled.

"You didn't come for that, though, did you?"

"I wanted to propose an alternative. My boss said I could if I figured you'd buy it."

"Put myself out as bait for Igorovitch?"

"Yeah, but it can't be that simple—"

"No!" Bess interrupted.

"Yes," Frost told her quietly. "If I set myself out as bait, then maybe he'll come for me when I expect him to. Otherwise, he could come anytime."

Plaskewicz sipped at his beer again, then began, "It's

not going to be that simple, anyway. He'll know we've warned you—I think he wanted it that way. He was in charge of security on the laser gun project for the KGB. You're the one who screwed him up. He wants you hard."

Bess whispered, "So do I."

Frost felt her squeeze his hand.

Chapter Thirty-One

It was a safe house, but a safe house with one hopefully very subtle lapse in security—subtle enough to draw Igorovitch and his team without warning him.

Frost sat on the veranda, watching the sun set, his wounds completely healed. He heard the click of heels behind him and reached down for the Metalifed High Power.

But it was Bess, bringing him a drink, her legs darkly tanned beneath the hem of the dark blue sundress, her shoulders and face tanned as well.

"Frost."

He took the drink—Seagram's Seven and ice with a splash of water. "Thanks, kid."

"When will they come, Frost?" She sat down on the chair opposite him, brushing her dress under her with her hands, looking down at it as she smoothed it over her legs, not looking at him.

"Soon—has to be soon."

"This house is expensive. Glad the government's picking up the tab," she laughed, still not looking at him.

"Aren't you drinking?"

"No—not for a while." She looked up finally, taking one of his cigarettes from the table and his lighter,

working the lighter two-handedly like women sometimes do, inhaling the smoke. She exhaled it through
her nostrils. "When is it going to end?"

"Soon for Igorovitch. Not for us."

"Frost!" She threw the cigarette down into the
ashtray, coming out of the chair, dropping to her bare
knees on the flagstones beside his chair, burying her
head against him. Frost held her tightly.

"Soon," he repeated, watching the orange orb of sun
shift down and away.

Frost opened his eye—the beeper beside the bed on
the nightstand was going. He punched it off, hitting the
switch. He sat up, Bess rolling over beside him.
"Frost?"

"It's them, kid," he told her.

"Oh, my God," she whispered.

Frost swung his feet out of the bed and to the floor.
On the chair on the other side of the nightstand were his
Levis. He started to pull them on, not bothering with
underpants.

"Where are you going?"

"Out—before they get here."

"But Plaskewicz and his men—"

"I'm not just sitting here, kid—to let Plaskewicz and
his guys maybe miss Igorovitch and we go through this
all over again."

"But that was the idea with the drainage ditch being
left unwired and this room being bombproof."

"He could still get us. Say maybe Igorovitch has
three guys or so with—aagh!"

"What is it?" Frost could see her silhouette in the

moonlight through the window.

"I caught the hair on my crotch in the damned zipper! Relax."

"Frost!"

"You wanna go through life sleeping behind bullet-proof glass or you want the windows open again—ever?"

"I want you!" She was out of bed, standing beside him. He could see her faintly in the gray light, the hem of her ankle-length nightgown swaying against the motion of her body. Her tiny fists were balled at her sides. "Be careful—be careful, Frost. I know you've gotta go."

Frost wrapped his arms around her, kissing her, then stepped into his shoes, barefooted. He pulled a knit shirt over his head, then dropped the Cobra Comvest diagonal rig over his shoulders, picking up the High Power from the nightstand.

He slipped the High Power into the shoulder holster, locking the thumbreak closed behind the hammer spur. He walked to the closet, reaching down for the KG-99, pulling the magazine, checking it, giving it a whack on the spine against the palm of his left hand, then reinserting it. He worked the bolt, then the safety.

He turned around and handed it to Bess. "Just in case this room isn't as assault-proof as they said it is and they get past me."

She didn't take the gun, throwing her arms around him instead.

He kissed her hard on the mouth, then pushed her away. "Lock the door—"

"Lock the door after you," she nodded in the gray light. "I know. Come back."

"I love you too, kid." He added, "That's why I'm goin'." He started for the door, snatching up his CAR-16 and his new Gerber knife. He stuck the Gerber's sheath into his trouser band in the small of his back, slinging the CAR cross-body under his right shoulder after adjusting it to the auto mode. He snatched up three extra magazines, ramming them into his belt under the shirt, the metal cold against his bare skin.

He tripped the deadbolts one after another, then opened the door, his hands working the CAR-16's bolt, chambering the top round. There was no one in the hallway that he could see.

"Lock it—and stay put," he ordered Bess, stepping into the hall and leaning against the wall as he heard the sounds of the bolts clicking closed.

He started down the hall, toward the stairs leading to the first floor, staying near the wall.

The one-eyed man didn't delude himself—he knew that he couldn't. The alarm Plaskewicz's men had tripped for him simply meant the system had picked up intruders near the ditch. It could have been a common burglar who got lucky. But it wasn't. Plaskewicz and his men could be moving, to stop Igorovitch before he got near to the house. But they wouldn't be. They'd let him get to the house, so they'd have a better chance of catching him. Frost realized too that his life, Bess's life—none of this mattered as much as getting Igorovitch into good killing ground. This was what Plaskewicz and his CIA people would want. This was why Frost was out in the dark with his guns rather than hiding with Bess in the comparative safety of the room. "Bomb-proof," he murmured. That was a contradiction of terms—the room could be "tamper-resistant" but never perfect. If Igorovitch got that far, he could get into the room as well.

Frost reached the head of the stairs, then started down, hearing something, wheeling.

"Captain Frost!"

It was one of Plaskewicz's men. Frost recognized the voice.

"You shouldn't be out, sir. Mr. Plaskewicz sounded the alarm and, well—you shouldn't be out."

"I know. That's why I'm out. Keep an eye on Miss Stallman—anything happens to her, you'll wish Igorovitch had gotten you." Frost kept walking, down the stairs without waiting for the man to say anything further.

He reached the base of the stairs, then started across the hall there.

"Captain Frost, Mr. Plaskewicz left orders—"

Frost wheeled on the man who already had a snubby Model 66 in his right fist. "You gonna stop me?" Frost asked matter-of-factly.

"No, sir. I was just pointing out—"

"Just keep an eye on the woman upstairs." Frost turned and kept walking.

He entered the library, stopping by the doors first to adjust his eye to the diminished light. Then he started across, toward the library doors leading to the veranda. He had memorized the route beginning the first night two weeks earlier when he and Bess had arrived.

He opened the library doors, the moonlight bright there, stepping through, quickly, then moving along beside the side of the house.

"Captain Frost!"

"Yeah—I know," Frost rasped back to the darkness.

He said nothing else, just moving as silently as he could to the end of the veranda. He flicked the safety onto the CAR-16 and let the rifle slip around behind his back, muzzle down, reaching up as he jumped. He hit the top of the veranda wall, pulling himself up, flipping over and down into the shrubbery beside it on the outside of the wall.

He moved the safety back to selective fire, hugging the wall as he moved, stopping to listen for sounds of Igorovitch, or of Plaskewicz's men bracing him. There was none of this.

The one-eyed man reached the end of the veranda wall, then made a fast, low run toward the pool, jumping a lounge chair and stopping in a low crouch beside the wooden utility cabinet where the pool-cleaning materials were kept.

He listened in the darkness—no sounds but the sounds of a south Georgia night. He kept moving, dodging around the utility cabinet, running the length of the pool beside the edge of the concrete apron and stopping beside the cabanas, waiting, smelling the night and chlorine from the pool—but hearing nothing.

He started ahead, past the pool and into the manicured garden, toward the fence line. But he crossed the garden at almost a diagonal, hugging the tree line as best he could, trying to intersect the road leading to the house.

The one-eyed man froze.

Submachine-gun fire sounded—muted and cough-like, the rattling of the bolt louder than the reports of the gun. And from behind him at the main house.

The one-eyed man started running, back toward the

house, hearing Plaskewicz shouting, "Frost—wait! Wait!"

The one-eyed man wouldn't wait. None of the CIA people had silenced subguns—it had to be Igorovitch.

"Frost, it was a trick. They ambushed Margaret Jenks! Don't you see!"

The one-eyed man stopped, Plaskewicz running up beside him. "I had to tell you they got Matt—you'd never have let Bess get set-up like you would yourself and—"

The one-eyed man snapped his right fist out, square to the center of Plaskewicz's face, Frost feeling the nose crush under his knuckles.

Then he started to run, toward the house, the gun-fire there.

"Bess!" He shouted it, his lungs burning with it as he crossed the garden, into the pool area, skirting the water's edge, past the border with the veranda and straight across. He hit the flagstone hard, an explosion ripping through the top floor of the house, glass tinkling as it rained down. Frost pushed himself to his feet.

He shouldered through the library doors and into the darkness there, a velvety blackness compared to the moonlight-bathed exterior of the house.

He froze again—a sixth sense making him feel something, someone. He threw himself forward, going into a roll, flashes of brightness in the darkness near the doors into the hall, the repeated coughlike sounds, the hammering of a bolt opening and closing.

Frost pulled himself across the floor and behind a desk, waiting.

To have shot toward the muted flashes would have

been to reveal his position for whoever waited in the darkness—Igorovitch.

"Captain Frost?"

The one-eyed man recognized the voice—the voice which had all but laughed as it set the mob of angry Pakistanis after him.

"Captain Frost?"

Frost didn't answer.

"We only have a moment. In Alaska I tried to kill Margaret Jenks—but not really. It was all to make them think I would take my revenge on the women of the men who undid me. And I knew the CIA would react as it did—tell you I was after you, purposely set things up to draw you out of the house so I could have a clear chance at your woman. But they did just what I wanted. You did just what I wanted. You're in my killing ground now."

The voice was like a rusty file being drawn across a chalkboard—and something like the one-eyed man imagined the devil might sound.

"Captain Frost, your time has come. Now, men."

The one-eyed man tucked down, flashes of light from all sides of him, gunfire thudding into the desk top and sides, into the paneling of the walls, lighting the room like a dim lamp. The pictures on the walls—he could hear the glass shattering, and the glass in the doors as well. He was trapped.

The gunfire kept coming, the one-eyed man knowing that in seconds a stray bullet would find him, and perhaps a shout or a gasp of pain would key his position and then it would be over.

As soundlessly as he could, the one-eyed man reached for the center drawer of the desk, pulling it an

200

inch or so open, the gunfire still coming, slivers of wood from the desk top pelting his fingers. He found a handful of rubber bands, then tucked his hand down. Frantically, in the darkness, half of them falling from his fingers, he strung the rubber bands together, then laced the string through the trigger guard of the CAR-16, the rubber bands long enough that he could hook them on the collapsed buttplate of the weapon. He tied them.

It was a gamble—something he didn't like to do. He was hoping that the power would still be on in the house.

He set the CAR-16's selector to full auto, raising the rifle clear of the desk top, holding it in his left hand by the base of the pistol grip, his right hand on the collapsed stock's buttplate.

The thing might not work at all.

He snapped back the buttstock, the weapon bucking in his hands on full auto, then threw the gun across the room toward the library doors leading into the hallway.

The flashes of the weapon were brilliant, sustained, the gunfire from around the room concentrating there. The one-eyed man jumped to his feet, took two long strides, almost falling over an overturned chair. He hit the wall, his left hand reaching out for the light switch that should be there, his right hand snatching for the Metalifed High Power under his left armpit.

The firing of his CAR-16 had ceased, the magazine empty.

Frost hit the switch, his eye closed, then wheeled, squinting against the light toward the library doors. His four assailants were in a ragged ring near the doors, their weapons trained in what had been total darkness in the direction of his rifle.

Frost pumped the trigger on the High Power, a fast two-round burst into the back of Igorovitch's neck, the man wheeling, dead as he collapsed toward the doors.

Frost fired the High Power again, two rounds to the nearest sub-gunner, moving the muzzle of his pistol onto the third man but realizing already that it was too late. The submachine gun the man held was already chattering, bullets thudding into the wall beside Frost's head.

There was a booming sound, then another and another, then a fuselade of heavy caliber handgun fire, the third and fourth sub-gunner dropping, the handgun fire subsiding.

Frost looked to the door leading to the veranda. There stood Plaskewicz—a sodden and blood red handkerchief pressed to the center of his face—and three other men, a variety of large and medium frame revolvers in their hands.

Frost rammed his High Power into his belt and started to run.

"Where the hell are you going?"

Frost didn't answer the nasal-sounding Plaskewicz, running across the hallway, taking the stairs to the second floor three at a time. "Bess!" he cried out.

He reached the second floor, the smoke there heavy and putrid. He reached the end of the corridor and their room. The body of one of the CIA men was there, burned, twisted, ripped apart from the force of the bomb.

The door still stood.

Frost hammered on it.

"Bess! Bess!"

The door opened a crack and all he could see was the muzzle of the KG-99 for an instant. Then the door opened wide, and Bess was there, her eyes frightened, but her mouth curving into a smile as she came into his arms.

"It really was bombproof," the one-eyed man whispered to her, but he didn't think she heard.

Chapter Thirty-Two

They had been back at the apartment on the outskirts of Atlanta for less than an hour, Frost spending most of the time on the telephone to Alaska, confirming that Margaret Jenks had not been killed despite the attempt on her life, that all the Jenks family—Matt, Margaret and their son—were alive and well.

Frost had left the house in south Georgia almost immediately, sharing the driving with Bess so they could each get at least an hour's worth of sleep. The 1978 Ford LTD was parked now, the essential luggage removed. He'd get the rest whenever he woke up.

It was already three A.M.

He set down the phone finally, Bess standing by the kitchen counter, opening mail, throwing most of it in the kitchen trash can.

"Frost?"

"They're fine—all of them. Matt has more surgery scheduled for the stuff Igorovitch did to him, but it should work out okay."

"Even if Plaskewicz lied to you—did you have to break his nose when you hit him?"

"Seemed like the thing to do at the time," Frost smiled, standing up, feeling stiff, walking toward the counter. He took a swallow of the drink Bess had poured him. The whiskey burned as it went down, warming him. Talking long distance to Alaska had made him feel cold—he knew that was stupid.

"Look at this."

The one-eyed man took the letter-sized envelope, the address almost obscured by the vast amount of stamps used. It was from Pakistan.

The one-eyed man tore it open. There was a letter and a folded-in-half photograph. He glanced at the photo—it was fuzzy. He looked at the letter. The handwriting was neat.

He read it aloud: "Captain Frost—All is well with my family here and my wife has crafted for me a new burnoose from the material which you so kindly purchased. My eldest son goes well at learning the ways of the sword so one day he too can serve to guard the Khyber Pass. On a recent excursion into less friendly climes I took the enclosed snapshot—of an old and unexpected friend. Look beyond the missing left arm— see the eyes as best as you can, Captain. They still have fire. The blessings of Allah to you and yours. Respectfully—Akbar Ali Husnain, Pathan of the Afridi tribe and guardian of the Khyber Pass."

Frost set down the letter, looking more closely at the photograph. Where it bent in the middle he could see a small figure, the left sleeve of the heavy coat hanging limp, an assault rifle in the clenched right fist.

"Here." Frost looked at Bess, then took the magnifying glass from her, squinting at the photo as he angled it against the overhead light. The face was all but obscured by the shawl which covered the hair—but he could see the eyes.

"It's Merana—alive," he murmured, feeling Bess

205

squeeze his hand. . . .

Frost held Bess close for a while, the sky brightening outside because it was near dawn. But he had no clock to awaken to. The fingers of his right hand traced across her abdomen, stopping at her left breast as he rolled over, holding her close to him.

He felt her lips touching at his neck, his face, her hands touching at his body, lingering, moving, returning. He watched the grayness through the curtains. In Afghanistan, men would be fighting—Subhan, Babrak ul-Raq, Hadji the hundred-year-old Buz Kashi rider. And a girl, too—Merana. He felt himself smile at the thought. Somehow she had survived, escaped, cheated death. He thought of Akbar—scholar, fighter, friend.

"What are you thinking about, Frost?" Bess whispered into his left ear.

"A lot of things—maybe a place I'll go back to sometime. I don't know, but it's a long way off."

"I'll make you stay," she murmured.

Frost slipped between her thighs, feeling the warmth there as he felt her hands against him.

He smiled—maybe she was right, but somehow the one-eyed man didn't think so.

THE SURVIVALIST SERIES
by Jerry Ahern

MORE FANTASTIC READING FROM ZEBRA!